About the _____

Hugh Canham has had two fulfilling careers: his first was as a solicitor with a central London law firm, where he became Managing Partner and briefly Chairman, during a period of great expansion when the firm had offices in Hong Kong, Los Angeles and Singapore. In the 1980s he switched his attentions to running a small farm in East Sussex and an antiques shop and gallery in Cranbrook in Kent with his wife. Hugh is the author of *The New Leaf*, published by Book Guild Publishing in 2014, and also several short stories. He now lives in London.

By the same author

The New Leaf, Book Guild Publishing 2014

LUCASTA
AND
HECTOR

Hugh Canham

Book Guild Publishing
Sussex, England

First published in Great Britain in 2015 by
The Book Guild Ltd
The Werks
45 Church Road
Hove, BN3 2BE

An earlier version of chapter 1 of *Lucasta and Hector* was published as a short story in Quadrant magazine in 2003.

Typesetting in Baskerville by
Ellipsis Digital Ltd, Glasgow

Printed and bound in Great Britain by
CPI Group (UK) Ltd, Croydon, CR0 4YY

A catalogue record for this book is available from
The British Library.

ISBN 978 1 910298 53 4

1

October 1969

'Hello, I'm Lucasta – I've come to sort out your books.'

The man in the heavy pinstriped suit looked puzzled. He peered through his thick glasses at the woman standing on his doorstep and then looked past her at the plane trees in the square as though the sight of their yellowing leaves might help him.

'You know, your father's books.'

'Ah! Of course! That sort of books. I thought you might be something to do with my accountants. Mind on the wrong track, you see. Come in, come in.'

He waved Lucasta past him into the splendid hall of the building. About 1780, Lucasta judged.

'This way, through the back. The books are in the library. Bit of a mess, I think you may find.'

The library must have originally been the room for entertaining in the house. Lucasta immediately imagined a line of ladies and gentlemen in eighteenth-century costume dancing a gavotte or whatever it was they did then. But this was only a passing fantasy. The reality was that the room, which was very large, had been lined out with mahogany bookshelves on three sides to house an extensive law library that seemed, at first glance, to contain old law reports, modern law reports, Hansard volumes, encyclopaedias and text-books, but it was all in considerable disarray, with many of the books lying open in untidy piles on the library table in the centre of the room as though someone had been searching for the answer to some obscure legal point, never found the answer and given up in despair.

At the end of the room she could see a carved mantelpiece and above it a large oil painting of a bewigged gentleman, presumably a judge, who seemed to be glaring at the mess on the library table. Underneath the portrait, completely obscuring the fireplace, were yet more mountains of books, piled high and falling about. These mountains continued in decreasing height for several yards until they became mere foothills as they reached the library table. And along the sides of the room were further piles of books, through which a pathway had been left to gain access to the bookshelves and the table.

'Goodness!' said Lucasta.

'Yes,' replied Hector, raising his eyebrows slightly. 'As you know, I should like you please to sort them out thoroughly. The law books should be put in order on the shelves, and the rest should be stacked subject by subject and probably sold. As Duncan no doubt told you, I'm hoping that there might be valuable stuff in this lot, particularly among the art books.'

'I'll make a start then,' said Lucasta. 'I'm glad I brought an overall – the books look rather dusty.'

'Quite so. Er, if you want anything I shall be in my office, off the hallway on the right.'

Lucasta put on her overall and then her glasses, and, taking a cursory look at the books, regretted she had taken the job. It had been Duncan, her fiancé, who had suggested it.

2

'I have to go to Hong Kong on business for two months, darling,' he had said one day out of the blue. 'I feel you may be bored while I'm away, so I wondered if you would like to take this temporary job I've heard about. It's for this friend of mine – I think you may have met him once at a party, a fishing pal of mine called Hector. He's just inherited his father's law practice somewhere off St. James's. It used to be a wonderful practice, wills and trusts for the gentry. Hector qualified as a solicitor with his father years ago, but then went off and joined a big firm in Lincoln's Inn. Never had to work very hard; I think he was just a salaried partner – spent a lot of his time fishing and shooting and looking at old churches. Anyway, his father had gone a bit ga-ga towards the end, it seems, and left everything in a bit of a mess, including his law library and a large collection of books – a lot of books on art, apparently. Hector asked me if I knew anyone who could help. Of course, I thought you would be ideal, what with your experience as a librarian and your art history degree. You'll be quite safe with Hector – he's more interested in himself than in sex.'

Duncan had beamed and chortled and puffed out his cigar smoke contentedly, and Lucasta thought that he could be a bit annoying at times. However, the next morning she had phoned Hector and arranged to take the job.

Lucasta was 28. People referred to her as 'a nice-looking girl'. She was small and thin with dark brown straight hair. She also had beautiful legs and a very large bosom which she was rather self-conscious about.

She started looking through the pile of books nearest to her. On the top and very dusty was a 1958

Chancery law report; next to it was what appeared to be a first edition of a novel by Kingsley Amis, then a copy of *The Nude* by Kenneth Clark, and finally two volumes of Bénézit – the dictionary of painters. There did not appear to be a paperback among them, as far as she could see. What a jumble! But she felt she simply couldn't start sorting the books without dusting them as she went along, and for that she'd need a large supply of dusters.

She walked down the hall and knocked tentatively on Hector's office door. Like the whole building, it was rather grand and intimidating. On hearing him call out 'Come in', she opened the door to find Hector seated behind a very large antique desk, reading *The Times*. A small fire was burning in the grate. There was a smell of tobacco.

'Ah, you've found something valuable already?'

'No, it's something much more prosaic. I'm going to need some dusters – the books are filthy.'

'Jolly has the dusters. He was Father's clerk and does more or less everything – I'll ring for him.'

But as his hand reached for an antiquated-looking intercom, his phone rang.

'Hector Elroy speaking . . . Yes, Your Grace . . . Yes, my father died three months ago and I have taken over his practice . . . An art theft? Of course, I will do anything to help. We have never met, but I knew the late Duke very well when I was young. I used to fish with him over a few days in the spring and again in the autumn . . . Of course, I can see you in half an hour.'

What a very large man Hector is, thought Lucasta, as he rose from behind his desk. He was obviously excited by his phone conversation and had forgotten all about the dusters.

4

'That,' he said, 'was the Duchess of Mercia. Wonderful that some of the old clients are still coming to the practice. My father had, as you will have gathered from the state of the books, let things go to the dogs. In fact, if it hadn't been for old Jolly keeping the trust accounts and things ticking over, I wonder what would have happened. As it is, I'm surprised the old man wasn't reported to the Law Society. I have inherited from him the lease of this wonderful house – which is where I now live – together with a run-down legal practice, not much money and an awful mess.'

Lucasta stood there not knowing quite what to say.

'However,' Hector continued, 'there's no time to lose. An art theft! An art theft! I know very little about art, but Duncan said you had a degree in art history. I think we should make you the practice's art expert, if you're in agreement. But why, I wonder, has the Duchess not gone to the police?'

Twenty minutes later the Duchess was shown into Hector's office by Jolly. Lucasta, feeling she had better go along with Hector's suggestion, had changed out of her overalls, washed her hands and – somewhat reluctantly, because Hector had asked her to 'smarten herself up a bit' – applied some lipstick and eye make-up. She sat in an armchair that Hector had positioned for her at the side of his desk.

The Duchess was probably not more than 50. She was dressed in a very elegant tweed suit and a short fur coat and appeared very nervous.

'Mr Elroy, I'm so pleased you could see me at such short notice,' she began, then, looking slightly flushed, said, 'Excuse me, I feel so warm in London after Scotland; do you mind?' At which she removed her fur coat and dropped it negligently on the floor. She then lit a cigarette and drew on it heavily. 'I am very, very worried, Mr Elroy. I don't know what to do.'

Hector adopted a Sherlock Holmes posture behind his desk, placed his hands together and said, 'Please just tell me what happened from the beginning. You told me it concerned an art theft, which is why I have asked my art expert, Lucasta Smith, to be present. You may speak quite freely in front of her and rely on her absolute discretion.'

The Duchess bowed her head graciously towards Lucasta and recounted the events leading to the theft.

'The grounds of our estate are, as you know, wild rather than formal, and decorated here and there with some fine statues dating from the nineteenth century. I have always loved contemporary art and constantly told the Duke we should have something more modern. Well, I was delighted when he bought me for our silver wedding a Henry Moore. Here is a photograph of it. It's a mother and child and very fine. I had it placed on a plinth on our top lawn not far from the house, within view of our bedroom window. The Duke left its siting entirely to me as it was a present, but he did stipulate that it was essential that it be securely fixed to the ground, the statue to the plinth and the plinth to the earth with spikes set in concrete, like all the other statues have been, otherwise the insurance he was arranging would be invalid.

'Our wedding anniversary was just after Easter and since then I have failed to have the fixing work done. On Sunday morning – that was yesterday, wasn't it? – I was horrified when I got up to find the statue missing from its plinth. Fortunately, the Duke is away until Wednesday night, but I am really terrified what he will say when he finds the statue gone. It undoubtedly cost a great deal and I'm afraid the Duke has a terrible temper. Things he refers to as "inefficiency" – he used to be in the Army, you know – particularly enrage him. I have not gone to the police about the theft because if they know, undoubtedly the Duke will have to know. I came down from Scotland on the night sleeper so as to see you as early in the morning as I could because your father was the only person I could think of who would have helped in a discreet way, so I hope you will do the same. Possibly you could arrange for a private detective or something? I'm prepared to offer a substantial reward if the statue can be recovered and in place again by the time the Duke returns. You see, I'm sure the only people who could have taken the statue were the members of a fishing party who fished our river last week. These fishing parties always stay at the inn in the village but have to drive through our grounds near to the house to get to the river. Here is a list of the names and addresses of last week's party – they all have to sign the fishing book in the lodge for our ghillie who helps them fish. Four of the six names are very familiar to me – they come every year – but two are completely new. The ghillie said they were Germans and a bit odd – two men, possibly brothers. The man who leads the party has been coming for some years. He's a bluff sort of man called Grimes who keeps a pub in Norfolk, and these two gave the pub as their address. It is only a surmise on my part, but I can't imagine anyone local wanting a Henry Moore statue, and anyway they would have to bring a large vehicle into the grounds to take it away. The fishing party had Land Rovers, one with a German number plate. The statue would easily fit in the back of a Land Rover, although it is about three and a half feet high and very heavy.'

The Duchess stopped to light another cigarette. Hector pursed his lips as he looked at the list he'd been given.

'Ah,' he said, 'I happen to know this pub in Norfolk – it's by a river, a backwater of the Norfolk Broads. We could of course employ a private enquiry agent, but frankly I don't know a good one. May I suggest that I go down to Norfolk this afternoon and see what I can find out, as time is of the essence? I can pose as a fishing enthusiast. That shouldn't be difficult, as I actually am one.'

He permitted himself as much of a short laugh as he thought was appropriate to the seriousness of the occasion.

'Mr Elroy, I am *so* grateful. I do hope that Miss Smith will go with you. I do so trust a woman's intuition in these things.'

'Of course she will, if you wish! But Your Grace, just one question. Is there any possibility that Mr Grimes or any of the others known to you could have stolen the statue?'

'They have been coming for many years, Mr Elroy. I have no grounds to think them dishonest. I am sure it must be these Germans.'

'And you said that nobody else had an opportunity to steal it?'

'As I have said, one would need a large and sturdy vehicle. It must have been stolen sometime on Saturday evening. It was there, I know, on Saturday afternoon. We have a gatekeeper, and I enquired of him, but he says no other vehicles apart from those belonging to the fishing party passed in or out on Saturday.'

'But he could have missed something or be lying.'

'Both things are possible, but unlikely.'

'Very well. All the evidence points to the Germans. We shall be on our way to Norfolk immediately after luncheon.'

Lucasta had been despatched off home by her new employer to get a quick lunch and pack a bag, and she was not really surprised when a little later he arrived to pick her up in a Rolls-Royce.

He had changed from his pinstripes into a checked tweed suit and drove in silence for most of the way to Norfolk as he said he wanted to think out what they should do and how they should do it. During the three-hour drive Lucasta therefore had the opportunity to study Hector in closer detail. His clothes looked a little crumpled over his large frame, but his shirt and tie were neat and clean. His hair was jet black and brushed straight back. His complexion was dark and it looked as though he was the sort of man who ideally should shave twice a day. She couldn't help but compare him with Duncan, who was short and small and hardly taller than she was, but always jovial, whereas Hector seemed very solemn and rather pompous.

When they were nearly at their destination he announced that he had a plan, and would like to discuss it with her. It was as follows:

They were to stay if possible at the pub kept by Mr Grimes. They must assume that he and the other members of the fishing party apart from the Germans were innocent of the theft and not implicated in any way. They were to find out the whereabouts of the two Germans. If they were still at the pub, she and Hector were to assume that the statue was still on the premises until proven otherwise. If the Germans had gone, they were to follow them, assuming Grimes knew where they had gone to.

Lucasta had to admit that she couldn't think of any better way to proceed.

They booked into the pub. A German-registered Land Rover was in the car park, but it did not appear to be weighed down with a heavy load. Nor did the English-registered one. Hector quickly elicited from Mr Grimes that the German owners of the Land Rover were indeed the brothers who came to the pub from time to time for the fishing. Grimes happened to have two vacancies on his week's salmon fishing party in Scotland and had asked them if they would care to join it. They were still staying at the pub as, on their way back from Scotland, they had started to fall ill with flu and had been in their room ever since. The doctor had been to see them.

From this information, Hector wildly surmised that the Germans were not brothers at all, but a pair of homosexual art dealers, and he was sure the statue must be hidden somewhere in or around the hotel. As it was very heavy and they were ill when they arrived, they must have concealed it somewhere rather than carried it up two flights of very steep and narrow stairs to their room, which was next to Hector's. Hector was very excited about all of this, but Lucasta found it difficult not to feel depressed. Being dragged off in this bizarre expedition was not what she had been expecting when she had taken the job to sort out some books. Hector annoyed her by asking her repeatedly if she had any 'intuitive feelings', as the Duchess had suggested she might because she was a woman. Well, she hadn't! She couldn't see much of the river as it was getting dark when they arrived, but it looked very grey and slow moving. The view out of her window was of marshes from which a mist was rising. The bedroom itself was not too bad, but the place was definitely a pub and not an inn and the downstairs smelt of stale beer and cigarette smoke.

At breakfast the following morning Hector was dressed in green plus-fours and a yellow cardigan, with socks to match.

He handed Lucasta a piece of paper, which she read with amazement. Across the top was written 'THE SEARCH', then:

1. Kitchen – me
2. Bar and cellars – me
3. Land Rovers – you
4. Other bedrooms and landlord's flat – you
5. Gardens, landing stage, outbuildings – both
6. Boathouses – both

'This is not necessarily the order we shall do them in,' he whispered. There was no need to whisper as the restaurant area was otherwise empty. 'Do you have any questions?'

'How do we do all this without arousing suspicion?' Lucasta asked.

'Ah. Thought of that! We pretend that you lost a brooch last night and we are searching around for it.'

'What – in the other bedrooms and the landlord's flat?'

'No, no. I'll tell you my plan for those areas in a moment, but this ruse will cover the gardens, the riverside, etcetera.' He waved his hand grandly. 'You know how it is, if you've lost anything you often can't remember where you walked the previous day.'

'Well, I didn't walk around the gardens or the river bank when we arrived as it was getting dark!'

'Never mind, never mind,' responded Hector, waving his hands impatiently. 'And with regard to the boathouses, we shall hire a rowing boat and go fishing. I've already spoken to Grimes about it.'

'And what about the other bedrooms and the landlord's flat?'

'Well, I think the bedroom the Germans occupy could be a problem, but while I was chatting to Grimes last night about hiring the boat, he let on that he admires you greatly – says you have a wonderful figure and all that. Apparently his wife has left him; funny, he seems a decent enough chap to me! But there we are – I'm sure he'll be only too pleased to show you anywhere you please, if you just ask him nicely. He was curious to know who you were. I just said you were one of my employees.'

Lucasta could hardly believe what he was doing when, as the waitress came, he whispered again, 'This is where I get a look at the kitchens,' and proceeded to tell the waitress that he wanted two eggs with his bacon fried in a particular way and he would come and show the cook how to do them. At which he strode off to the kitchen, winking at Lucasta as he went.

The rest of the morning continued in much the same pantomime-like way. Lucasta felt a complete idiot pretending to be looking for a non-existent lost brooch in the flower beds. How could a three-and-a-half-foot statue be hidden in a flower bed?

'It could be in the middle of a shrub, or even decorating the flower bed,' said Hector. 'You know, we must look everywhere!'

Neither did Lucasta enjoy rowing up the river while Hector pretended to fish with the rod he'd brought with him, and even less the visit to the other bedrooms and to Mr Grimes' flat.

She met Hector in the bar at lunchtime. He had just been shown round the cellars by the barman.

'Come on, I know it's a bit chilly, but let's take our drinks outside,' he muttered. 'I presume you have drawn a blank like me, otherwise you would be smiling.'

Lucasta shrugged her shoulders. 'Well, I had a pretty good look round everywhere. Grimes was quite happy to show me anything provided I put up with his straying hands as we went round. When we got to his own flat, though, I thought I was going to have to fend off a rape, but the lecher contented himself with stroking my jumper and saying, "You've got a wonderful figure!" Goodness, I think I should get a percentage of the reward, in the highly unlikely event of our finding this blessed statue!'

'Good God, Lucasta – I'm awfully sorry!'

'Tell me,' she said, 'is finding the statue very important for you?'

'Very.'

'Why?'

'Well, first there's the reward, which is substantial. Secondly, I'm very worried about my father's old clients going somewhere else now that I've taken over the practice. It's vital that I keep the Duke and Duchess as clients – they have three large trust funds and two charities, all set up in England. Their fees pay all the overheads of the practice and provide a small income as well. I suppose without that work there would be nothing really substantial left!'

And at this point Lucasta's better nature prevailed. She felt sorry for Hector as he stood there looking rather pathetic in his green plus-fours and yellow socks.

'Very well. I'll try to get a look at the Germans' room, even if it is only a peep. I'll pretend I've come to measure for new curtains. They may not fall for it, but I do have a tape measure with me.'

She had brought it with her to measure the boot of the Rolls, to see if the statue would go in. (It would, just – diagonally – in the unlikely event of their finding it.)

Hector said that was a jolly good idea, and very brave of her, and he would be lurking in the corridor in case there was any trouble.

The curtain plan was a total failure. When Lucasta knocked on the Germans' door, she was confronted by a very large blond man in pyjamas, who had a very good grasp of English. He informed her that he did not want anyone near as he had the flu, and that the curtains were fine as they were. Then he slammed the door in her face.

After that, they both knew they were running out of time. Lucasta didn't quite know why, but she was becoming emotionally involved in it all against her will.

They came to the conclusion that the Germans must have disposed of the statue on the way down from Scotland, presumably to a colleague who would take it to the continent.

What more could they do? Nothing, it seemed – but Hector insisted on staying another night, 'just in case something turns up'.

'What other recourse do we have?' he asked.

'We could pray?' Lucasta said jokingly.

When she later met Hector in the bar for a drink before dinner, she realised that he had had several already – his face was red and he was muttering incoherently to himself. The dinner was even worse than the previous night's, although she didn't think Hector noticed as he drank almost all of the bottle of wine he ordered. After they had eaten, he asked if Lucasta would please wait up while he had a cigar with his coffee. In the bar there was a very noisy darts match being played, so they retired as far away from it as possible and sat on two small seats in a corner. Hector then announced that he needed a cognac with his coffee. She noticed that it was a very large one when he brought it back to where they were sitting.

He rambled on rather inconsequentially about the country's transport problems for some time, and Lucasta began to want badly to go to sleep. Then he said suddenly, 'Must go to the loo,' and lurched towards a nearby door which she remembered led onto a rather smelly yard where there was a gents' lavatory and where all the empty crates and barrels were stacked. She had only looked round that area very cursorily during their search because she couldn't bear the smell, but she had got Hector to inspect the loo later.

When Hector reached the door leading out to the yard he almost fell through it, he was so unsteady on his feet, and Lucasta felt she ought to follow him to see if he was all right. Once outside, she was just in time to see him trip again and fall sideways into the stack of empty metal beer barrels against the wall. There was the most awful crash as the barrels fell everywhere. She ran over to see if Hector was hurt, but by the time she reached him he was sitting up and looking at the wall against which the barrels had been stacked, transfixed.

'Look, look!' was all he said, pointing.

They had found the statue.

The first thought that flashed through Lucasta's

mind was that she had been very careless in her
search. She should, of course, have investigated the
empties. Oh dear!

'We've got to get it into the boot of the Rolls
a.s.a.p.,' said Hector, rising unsteadily to his feet. 'Go
and get it and back it round here pronto.'

'But . . . but Hector, I've never driven a Rolls!'

'Just get on with it, girl,' he said, handing her the
keys.

Given her lack of experience, she was surprised she
didn't dent the Rolls or knock down a wall. However,
she eventually made it round to where Hector was sitting on two upended barrels and by now seething, as
he tried to hide the statue with his body. Amazingly,
nobody had come out of the pub to see what the noise
was all about. It must have been drowned by the din
of the darts match.

'Get the boot open,' he said. 'We must somehow lift
it in.'

Lucasta took off her jacket and tried to lift the
statue. She could only move it about an inch.

Luckily, three youths, no doubt members of one of
the darts teams, were leaving the gents'. But they
looked almost as unsteady as Hector. How, Lucasta
thought, do darts players throw their darts so accurately when they have drunk so much beer?

'Would you kindly give this young lady and myself a
hand with this thing into the boot of my car?' said
Hector.

The youths, without showing any surprise or asking
any questions, but with much grunting and swearing,
got it into the boot. They were quite unconcerned
about the removal of the statue or why it was there,
and almost as unconcerned at the large tip Hector

handed them.

'Drive off fast,' Hector ordered Lucasta, getting into the passenger seat.

As Lucasta drove off, she noticed in the driving mirror that the youths had started to play some sort of football game with one of the empty beer barrels.

'Can't we collect our clothes?' she asked as they rejoined the car park.

'Too dangerous! Just drive straight to Scotland.'

'But which way do I go?' she asked in a panic.

'You see that compass on top of the dashboard? Keep it heading north until you come to the coast, then turn left. You should eventually come to the A1. By that time I shall have come round, but I need a doze now.'

And with that he dropped off to sleep. He had apparently forgotten that he wanted to go to the loo.

Lucasta had not gone very far when she realised she was being followed. As she wasn't sure which way she was to go, she began turning off down lanes that she thought would lead northwards, but whenever she turned, the headlights of the car behind followed.

She came to a town called North Walsham and drove straight into the centre of it. By the street lights she could see that the following car was a Land Rover. There were fortunately still a few people around, so she stopped. The Land Rover drove past and stopped some thirty yards ahead. It was, she noticed as it passed them, Grimes behind the wheel!

'Why have we stopped?' asked Hector sleepily.

'Because we are being followed – by Grimes!'

'Good God! Where is he?'

'Parked about thirty yards ahead. I think he must know we've taken the statue. What do we do?'

'Well, there are various alternatives.' Hector was

now wide awake. 'First, I could go and talk to him. Secondly, we could call the police – but Her Grace didn't want the police involved, and also we might not get the reward if we do – and third, and I think this is my preferred choice, we could try and give him the slip. We'll drive off in the direction of Cromer. It's a good straight road out of town. We'll endeavour to outpace him and turn down a side road. I'll drive now – I'd love to have a pee. A side road would be ideal.'

So Hector took over the wheel and drove off slowly, noticing that the Land Rover started off too, and followed them at a discreet distance. Once they were out of the town the road was very good and Hector was soon up to 80 mph in spite of the weight of the statue in the boot. Grimes soon dropped out of sight behind. Very soon Hector turned off to the left and drove down a lane for about a hundred yards, then stopped, turned off the engine and the lights, got out and relieved himself by the hedge in the dark. All was quiet as he returned.

'I think that's given him the slip,' said Hector complacently. 'I don't know the lanes around here so I think it best if we turn back and rejoin the main road. Hopefully, he will be tearing after us towards Cromer, trying to catch us up.'

Hector turned the Rolls around in a field gateway with some difficulty and made his way back to the main road, where he turned left. The road was completely clear.

Lucasta felt very nervous. The sight of Grimes' face behind the wheel of the Land Rover had not been pleasant.

'I do hope he doesn't turn round and come back,' she said. 'He could have a gun.'

'A bit far-fetched, I think,' said Hector. 'Anyhow, let's deal with that as and when it happens. I'm enjoying this. Much better than legal practice.'

Lucasta felt she would much rather be safely in bed in her flat. She started to cry. Hector merely passed her a handkerchief.

Soon the headlights flashed on a sign by the side of the road – 'Welcome to Cromer: Gem of the Norfolk Coast'. The streets were totally deserted.

'There's a one-way system here, I think. We have to go round to the left.'

No sooner had Hector said this than they both saw a Land Rover hurtling towards them from the part of the one-way system they could not enter.

'He's going to try and ram us,' shouted Hector. 'He must be mad or drunk.'

As they swung left into the one-way system, the Land Rover tried to come alongside them on their right. The road was narrow. Hector just accelerated as hard as he could. There was a slight thump as the left-hand front of the Land Rover hit the right-hand rear of the Rolls. For a moment Hector thought he was losing control as the Rolls swung to the left, but he turned the steering wheel to the left and righted the car. The Land Rover, totally off course, went straight into a lamp post.

Lucasta found herself screaming. Her legs were shaking and she felt sick.

'We must stop and see if he's all right,' she said. 'Hector, you *must*.'

Hector looked over his shoulder at the next turn but drove on.

'He deserved it,' he said. 'If we stop now we shall never get the statue back in time as the Duchess has commissioned us to do.'

'But he may be dead.'

'Well, if he is, there is nothing we can do about it.'

Lucasta lay back and groaned.

'This is terrible,' she said. 'I hate it.'

'Well, you always said you hated Grimes. We've got the statue and he's got his comeuppance. I look forward to reading in the *Cromer Gazette*, if there is such a thing, the headlines: "Drunk publican crashes Land Rover into lamppost".'

Lucasta just glared at him. 'You think it's funny, don't you?'

'No, I think it's part of the job we were asked to do. Tell you what, if it will cheer you up, you've been very brave and helpful and I'll share the reward with you fifty-fifty.'

Lucasta fell silent as they made their way along the coast road. After some time, as they were passing through Cley-next-the-Sea, she asked, 'How much is it?'

'Two thousand.'

'And I'm to get a thousand?'

'That's it.'

'I do hope he's not seriously injured,' she said, and went to sleep.

2

December 1969

For Lucasta, returning to the piles of dusty books was a great anti-climax. Although she'd been frightened by the car chase, it had been like the end of a romantic film when they delivered the statue to the Duchess. She had been so grateful to them both as she shook hands with an unshaven Hector and hugged and kissed Lucasta. Hector had given Lucasta a cheque for half the reward, which she left in her handbag for a week and kept looking at as though she couldn't believe it. She felt she'd achieved something of merit at last. She'd always been envious of her younger and more beautiful sister Veronica, who had won all the prizes at school, gone to Cambridge, and was now doing a doctorate, while all Lucasta herself had done had been to make various false starts. First, she'd tried a course at an art college until she decided that she was never going to be a good artist. Then she did a degree in the history of art, but that didn't seem to qualify her for any particular job, so she'd then taken a course to qualify as a librarian. Being a librarian was all right, but not exactly exciting. She'd worked in a university departmental library, but after a year had had to give in her notice because she couldn't stand her boss. Fortunately, the next day she met Duncan.

He seemed to be *the answer*. He had a good job in property development and was eager that they should get married quickly and have a family. She knew Duncan was not perfect – not only was he short, but he was round and chubby – but he was always happy and cheerful. Now she was missing him badly as she sorted through the dusty books. He'd promised to phone her twice a week, but he'd only rung once so far and they'd been cut off after about a minute. He'd said she couldn't contact him because he would be moving around and might have to go to the New Territories.

And Hector seemed to be staying away from her. The only person she saw while she worked on the books was Jolly, who kept her supplied with dusters. He annoyed her. He crept about, was obsequious, but seemed somehow to resent her presence in the office, and he was always dressed in the same pinstriped trousers with a shiny black jacket.

But eventually she had an excuse to speak to Hector on the intercom.

'Hector? Lucasta here. The first lot of books is now ready to be sold,' she said brightly. 'Would you like to come and look at them?'

'No, no, I'm happy to leave it all to you.'

'Very well – but can you please tell me two things? First, why are all these books open on the table? And, secondly, why did your dad buy all these books – particularly the art books? Some of them have wonderful reproductions and must have cost a small fortune. Did he buy pictures, too? I've never seen any around the office.'

'No, he never bought a single picture. He visited the galleries regularly and I suppose he just liked looking at the books. It's very odd, isn't it? He seems to have developed an obsession with buying books. I believe it's quite a common obsession, and he would never let Jolly tidy anything in the library. He said it might interfere with a legal point he was looking up. I'm sorry you've got such a muddle to sort out, but I have one, too – the filing system is in chaos. In fact, the only things that are in order in the office are the trust accounts and the firm's ledgers, which Jolly dealt with.'

After this conversation Hector went back to wondering yet again what his father had done with all the money he must have drawn out of the practice. If he had known how little cash he would inherit from his father he would have not been so eager to leave the firm in Lincoln's Inn. It had paid him very well and he had been asked on leaving to give an undertaking not to solicit any of the firm's clients for a period of eighteen months. Most of them were gentleman farmers or the owners of substantial estates, and friendship with them had been the basis of his social life as a bachelor. Normally, he would at this time of the year be out shooting two or three times a week. But now he felt he had to refuse all the invitations, and just went to his club for lunch and dinner each day, spending the rest of his time trying to sort out his father's piles of belongings. He was finding it a melancholy and difficult business deciding what pieces of his furniture from his rooms in Piccadilly to bring to his father's house. He'd always looked forward to living in the house in St. James's Square, ever since the day his father had said to him, just after he'd finished his Articles with him, 'You know, my boy, there's not really enough work here for two qualified people. I've made arrangements with my old friend Mitchell in Lincoln's Inn to give you a job until I retire. Then, of course, you can take over the house and practice.'

Well, that had been twenty years ago, and his father had kept putting off retiring – no doubt, Hector thought, because he could not bear the thought of living in the country with Hector's mother – until, eventually, he died.

No new work was coming in and he was not allowed to advertise for it. But it occurred to him that he could advertise his services as an art theft investigator. So he placed an advert in one of the 'art world' magazines and, much to his amazement, as no sooner had it been published than he received an enquiry, and on the same day a cheque from the book dealer for £350 for the first lot of his father's books that Lucasta had sold.

'Thank you so much, Lucasta,' Hector said as he walked into the library. 'I've just had this cheque . . . Goodness! What on earth are you wearing?'

To counteract the dust from the books, Lucasta had taken to wearing a boiler suit, a face mask and a plastic shower cap while working on them.

'It's the dust!' she explained.

'As bad as that? Good heavens! Well, anyhow, I've just come to thank you for this cheque and ask if you would be prepared to accompany me on a trip to Yorkshire. An artist chap phoned. He's trying to prepare for an exhibition, but somebody keeps stealing his pictures as soon as they're finished. He's asked me to investigate.'

'Why not the police?'

'He tells me he smokes pot while he paints and the studio reeks of it – so not a good idea to involve the police!'

'Is he well known?'

'Never heard of him myself, but *he* says he's well known – name's Melvin Delaney.'

'Oh! *I* know him. He taught us life drawing at art college.'

'Er, I didn't know you'd been to art college. That's different from your art history degree, is it?'

'Completely. At first I thought I wanted to be an artist, but I was useless and dropped out after a year. I then did the degree.'

'I see . . . Well, apart from the dust, is everything all right?'

'No – it's cold in here,' Lucasta replied, hugging herself. 'I keep asking Jolly if he could turn up the heat in the radiators and he says "Yes miss", but they never seem to get any hotter.'

'Oh dear. The central heating is very antiquated. I've got a fire in my office and in my sitting room. I'll buy you a convector heater, shall I?'

'That would be very nice!'

'So – are you willing to come to Yorkshire with me?'

'Oh yes. It will be a change from the dust and the books, and maybe a bit warmer than this library at present!'

'Well, I don't know that Yorkshire is noted for its warmth,' Hector mused. 'I went grouse shooting once in September near the place where Delaney says he lives and it was freezing! By the way, I think we'd better travel by train. If we arrive in the Rolls he'll think we're going to overcharge him! We can apparently get a taxi from the station, which is only five miles away, and there's a good hotel in the village to stay at.'

'Let's hope it's better than the pub in Norfolk!'

It turned out to be considerably better. And the next morning they made their way across the village green to Melvin Delaney's house, which was on the outskirts of the village. It was now nearing Christmas and there had been a hard frost overnight. Lucasta was very glad that she'd brought her woolly hat and gloves with her, as well as a thick overcoat. Hector did not seem to feel the cold, she noticed. All he had on was a stout tweed three-piece suit, a cap and a scarf round his neck. Lucasta had a small bet with herself that Melv – as he was always known amongst the students – would not remember her. He had had a reputation for asking several of the more forward girls to pose for him in the nude privately, but he'd never asked her. She remembered at the time that she'd been a bit disappointed – he obviously did not think she was beautiful enough!

It must have been eight or nine years since she'd seen Melv. Once they managed to get to see him, he struck her as looking odder than ever. The front door of his very substantial stone-built house was opened by a young lady wearing a massively thick, long jumper and a very bad-tempered expression on her face.

'Ah,' said Hector, not being able to decide at first glance if this was Melvin's wife, sister, daughter or domestic help. 'We've come to see Melvin Delaney. He's expecting us.'

'What's it about?' snapped the young woman.

'Er . . . well, about some pictures.'

'Well, it would be I suppose. He's in his studio in the garden. Go straight down the hall and out the back door and you'll see it. You'd better knock. He usually has some naked woman in there.'

'Not very welcoming!' Hector muttered out of the corner of his mouth as they walked down the long hallway to the back of the house. 'Is that his wife?'

'I've no idea.'

'But I thought you said you knew him . . .'

26

'Yes, nine years ago. I don't think he was married then. Anyway, he was always asking young girl students to pose for him in the nude.'

'Did he ever ask you?'

'No, never. I don't suppose I was the right type.'

'Strange – I should have thought . . . but never mind; here we are. What a weird-looking place!'

The studio was about twenty-five yards from the house. It was a rustic-looking wooden building with a very high sloping roof made of glass. Hector knocked on a small low door which led into it, and as there was no response, opened it a crack and shouted, 'Mr Delaney? We're here as promised – Hector Elroy and assistant.'

'Damn! Come in I suppose.'

'Another warm welcome!' muttered Hector.

Melvin Delaney, heavily bearded and clad in cords and an artist's smock with a scarf round his neck, turned from the easel and beckoned them in. On a chaise longue beside the easel there reclined a naked and very well-rounded young lady with bright red hair that came down almost to her waist.

'We've visitors, Aggie, so cover up your goose pimples my dear and go across to the house, warm up and make yourself a cup of tea or something until I shout for you again.'

Aggie got up, coughed, covered herself with a dirty-looking dressing gown and, pausing only to light a cigarette, vanished into the frosty garden in bare feet.

'Sorry to greet you so crossly,' said Melvin, starting to fill a pipe from a jar of tobacco near his paints, 'but I'd just got to a difficult bit. Aggie is a lovely girl but she won't keep still, particularly when she's cold. I try to heat this place up as much as I can, but it's difficult in winter.'

'Shall we talk here or would you rather go into the house?' said Hector. 'This, by the way, is Lucasta, my assistant.'

Melvin glanced at Lucasta keenly and raised his eyebrows.

'I see,' was all he said enigmatically. 'We'd better stay here so that you can find some clues as to how these bloody pictures keep disappearing! You can see the ones that haven't been nicked standing in a line against the wall over there. They're all the same size as the one I'm working on – seven feet by four. The first three are of my wife, Molly, but she caught a chill and then developed bronchitis and had to stop posing – said it was due to the cold in here, of course! I was frantic – the exhibition is opening on the 5th of January, so I had to find an alternative model. Aggie is quite good, but she can only come on Wednesdays and Fridays. I've got June for the other days. She's more flexible, but not so good. Frankly, neither of them is professional and they keep fidgeting. It makes me very bad tempered. Anyhow, somehow I managed to bash off a few more pictures, and then I noticed that some were missing. I'm desperate to get them back, you see – I need at least twenty for the exhibition.'

'When did you first notice that some pictures were missing?'

'The day I phoned you. God, I was nearly demented!'

'Have the paintings that have disappeared been of both your models?'

'No, that's the odd thing – I think they're all of Aggie. Well, no, some pictures of June may have gone, too. I'm not sure. Certainly none of the ones I did of Molly have gone.'

'Don't you number your paintings?'

'No. Never have.'

'How could the pictures be removed from here?'

'Well, they could only be taken out through those big doors at the end there. The one you came in by is too small. The big doors lead out into our orchard and then you can get round by the side of the house into the road. I used to leave the studio unlocked, but after the theft of the first picture I've kept both the doors locked!'

'And where are the keys kept?'

'I try to keep them in my pockets, but the key to the big doors is a bloody enormous thing and I sometimes take it out and put it down somewhere.'

'And what do you do with the keys at night, when I presume the pictures were taken?'

'Right! Well, I take the keys out of my pocket and chuck them down somewhere in the bedroom.'

'So it would have been possible for someone to grab them from there and have them copied?'

'Possibly, but look, that's what I want you to find out!'

'Of course, you could simply change both the locks.'

'I'm going to do that, but I want to find out what bastard would do this to me!'

'Do you have any enemies?'

'Nobody round here seems to like me very much. Apparently the Free Church minister says publicly from his pulpit that I'm a corrupter of morals.'

'Why is that?'

'Because I paint nudes, of course. But he's a silly sod!'

'Would there be anyone jealous of you painting their wife or girlfriend in the nude?'

'Aggie's husband is a local shepherd. I pay her well and they need the money. June is more or less the local tart, so I don't think anyone would be jealous of her!'

'I see. No sign of anyone breaking into the studio or the house?'

'No.'

'Do you mind if we have a look around?'

'Help yourselves; go where you like. I'm going indoors now. Come into the kitchen when you're finished.'

Hector noted that the key to the big double doors was indeed very large and heavy. He took it out of the lock and put it in his jacket pocket. It felt very uncomfortable.

'Did you smell the pot?' he asked Lucasta when they were outside.

'No – well, actually, I'm not sure what pot smells like, believe it or not. I've always steered clear of drugs.'

'He probably smokes that foul pipe to try and cover up the smell of the pot. Anyway, I think that's irrelevant. Let's look round the outside of the studio and have a general stroll around. I wonder what the thief does with the pictures, you see. They must be very difficult to carry. Ha!' They had now reached the end of the orchard. 'The remains of a bonfire – maybe, of course, from Guy Fawkes night. Look over there, in that lean-to shed – a paraffin can, and also what I need for my search – a leaf rake!'

'Whatever for, Hector?'

'Well, I may be completely mistaken – or barking up the wrong tree, as one should say in an orchard . . .'

He didn't finish what he was saying, but grabbed the rake and started very carefully to pull it through the ashes of the bonfire. As he seemed not to wish to communicate what he was hunting for to Lucasta, she went over to the lean-to shed and sat down on a small rickety bench inside it. That joke about the 'wrong tree' was just typical of Hector. He was all right when you got to know him and she could see why Duncan and he were friends, although Duncan was a much more jolly and open person. She suddenly wondered whether Duncan had perhaps written her an airmail letter and that would be waiting for her when she got back home. But she put that thought away as, after several exclamations of 'Ha!', Hector was now approaching her with several small objects in his outstretched palm.

'I think we're on the right track. Tell me, are these the sort of things with which you attach a canvas to a stretcher?'

'Possibly,' said Lucasta dubiously.

'And is this not a piece of charred canvas?'

Lucasta examined it closely. 'Looks very like it,' she said.

'Well then, it seems to me that the paintings were burnt on the bonfire.'

'But wouldn't people see the flames if it was done at night?'

'Maybe. But I suppose if you smothered the canvas in paraffin and set fire to it with a few newspapers it would soon be gone.'

'Even quicker if you use petrol.'

'Very good, Lucasta! Shall we open the can and have a sniff? . . . You're right, it's petrol! Well, I think we must be right!'

'Well, it may explain how the pictures were disposed of, but not who did it.'

'True, but I think it must be an inside job. What did you think of the nudes he's finished, by the way?'

'Excellent. He always was talented, but very strange.

I particularly like the way he blurred the faces so that it was just a body.'

'Oh, that's good is it?'

'I thought so.'

A few minutes later they were in Melvin's large kitchen which had an Aga in it so it was reasonably warm. Aggie was sitting by it in a broken-down Lloyd Loom chair, huddled in her dressing gown. Melvin was standing at the kitchen table holding a large china jug.

'Cider anyone? Home made from the apples in the orchard. Chap down the road has got an even bigger orchard and a cider press. Very useful. Tell me what you think of it!'

Lucasta thought she would have preferred a cup of hot tea or coffee, but as she was not offered one she drank the cider. It seemed very warming, and after a second glass had been pressed upon her she started to feel very sleepy. She told herself it must be because she'd come into the warmer kitchen from the cold outside and took off her coat and hat. In the background she could hear Hector explaining how he'd found the staples and the piece of canvas and she heard Melvin saying, 'Good work, good work. We'll get the bugger!' And then she must have dozed off.

She woke up when she felt someone patting her hand. For a moment she wondered where she was and then she saw that Melvin was standing over her trying to wake her up.

'Come on, Lucasta – not used to strong cider! You look very pretty with a pink flush on your face.'

Lucasta looked round the kitchen. Aggie and Hector were no longer there – it was just her and Melv.

'Goodness, your cider's strong, Melvin. I thought you didn't remember who I was when we first came.'

'Of course I did. I always remember lovely girls who've been my pupils. You shouldn't have given up, you know. You could have been quite good!'

'But not *very* good!'

'I always wanted to ask you to pose for me, you know, but I knew you'd refuse and I hate being rejected. But now you're with this Hector chap I suppose you're less prudish than you seemed nine years ago.'

'I'm not sleeping with Hector, Melvin! I just work for him.'

'How strange . . . but, well, how about it? You always had the most gorgeous tits and they look even better now.'

'Certainly not.'

'Oh, come on. Let me have a closer look. They're lovely!'

Lucasta was about to take evasive action when there was a most horrific crash behind her as the door into the kitchen from the hall was thrown open, hitting the kitchen dresser which was full of plates, and dislodging several of them, which broke into pieces on the stone floor.

'You miserable lying and cheating bastard!' a voice shrieked.

Lucasta looked round and there was the young woman who'd opened the front door to them when they'd first arrived, now looking dementedly angry.

'I heard every word you said to this girl just now. You're disgusting and I hate you!'

'Now, now, Molly. Don't get so angry. I can explain everything,' said Melvin, backing away.

'You bloody well can't, and you won't.' At which

33

Molly picked up the jug that had held the cider and hurled it at Melvin's head. It missed, crashing against the Aga and falling to the floor in several pieces. 'You said when you married me that you'd never sleep with another of your models. You said I was the perfect model and you'd never want a better, didn't you? I know what you've been doing with that Aggie girl with the red hair. That's why I burnt your paintings of her. You fool! Fancy calling in a detective!'

Lucasta quietly slipped out of the kitchen and into the hall, where she immediately met Hector.

'What on earth is happening?' he said to the sound of further china breakages.

'His wife is throwing things at him and has just confessed to burning the pictures because she was jealous of Aggie. I think our job is done. Goodness, I feel woozy!' replied Lucasta.

'Yes, so do I. Melvin told me to look round the house if I wanted to. Frankly, I went outside to get some fresh air.'

'Well, it sounds as if she's trying to kill him.'

'Had we better try to intervene?'

'No, let's get out!'

By the time they had checked out of the hotel, ordered a taxi and boarded the train heading for London they both felt a good deal better.

'Remind me not to drink home-made cider again,' said Hector, rubbing his face. 'That's enough alcohol to last me till Christmas. Such a simple solution to Melvin's problem. Strange he couldn't see it for himself, but I suppose the combination of the pot and the home-made cider numbs the thought processes. But you say his paintings were very good!'

'Most good artists seem to be half-drunk most of the time!'

'Ah, well!' sighed Hector.

And they then discussed for the second or third time the question of who really had stolen the Duchess's statue and what whoever had stolen it intended to do with it. But they came to no conclusions about it all.

Then Hector said, 'I'm so sorry about the violence again this time, Lucasta. Quite unexpected. Duncan will be very cross with me for getting you into these scrapes. I suppose he'll be home for Christmas?'

'I don't know. I haven't heard from him recently.'

'Oh dear. Why not?'

'I don't know. He phoned once shortly after he went away, but we were cut off after a minute or so and I haven't heard from him since. I expect he'll write. He said he'd been moving around. If he doesn't come back I'll just have to go home on my own for Christmas. It's always terribly holy. Dad's a clergyman, you see!'

Lucasta did not tell Hector what Melvin had said to her that had first caused Molly's fury. But she did raise the question again of going back to Norfolk to try and retrieve their things from Grimes' pub.

'Definitely not, Lucasta. *Quieta non movere*.'

'But I left a very nice skirt and jumper there!'

'Never mind. Buy some new ones with your share of the reward.'

Thinking she must look up what *Quieta non movere* meant, she took the Tube back to her flat in Kensington, hoping there would be a letter from Duncan awaiting her. But there was nothing. She firmly decided she would not phone Duncan's London office. She'd met Duncan's best friend there several times and she was sure he would have contacted her if Duncan had met with an accident or anything like that. No, she would try to blank Duncan from her mind and go and spend Christmas as cheerfully as possible with her parents in their gloomy Victorian Gothic vicarage near Oxford.

'Hello darling, Veronica's here. So sorry Duncan's still away. We should have liked him to join us for Christmas, you know,' said her mother by way of greeting. 'Your father's very pleased with himself because, as I told you, he's been made a canon of the cathedral and you will notice he now wears his new cassock with the purple piping all the time, except when he goes to bed.'

Lucasta's father was an Anglo-Catholic and on Christmas Eve Lucasta and her sister had to sit through a very lengthy Midnight Mass with a small orchestra, as well as another long, solemn Mass on Christmas morning. Canon Smith had been so busy since Lucasta had arrived on the afternoon of Christmas Eve that he only got round to speaking to her at the Christmas lunch table.

'Pity your young man couldn't join us. What's his name again?'

'Duncan, Dad. You met him – remember?'

'Ah, yes. Tubby little fellow!'

'That's him!'

But Lucasta's sister Veronica was much more forthright.

'Didn't Duncan phone you before Christmas? I thought he was supposed to be back by now.'

'Yes, he was. And no, he didn't phone.'

'Mmm. If you ask me, he's found a little almond-eyed beauty to spend Christmas with in Hong Kong!'

Lucasta felt a strange lurch in the pit of her stomach.

'And how are things with you?' she asked.

'Wonderful. I've seduced my PhD supervisor. He's about sixty but *very* virile. I'm also having an affair with a first-year undergraduate called Paul. He's lovely. Got long hair and flared trousers. Very naïve and sweet.'

'Do you really like that sort of thing?'

'Of course, otherwise I wouldn't do it. You ought to break out a bit, Lu. What's this friend of Duncan's that you're working for like, by the way?'

'Well, Duncan, as you know, is hardly trendy. No long hair or flared trousers for him. But Hector looks as though he's stepped out of the 1950s, or even '40s! He's a middle-aged bachelor solicitor; smokes cigars and goes to his club a great deal. But he's all right when you get to know him a bit. No groping, thank goodness.'

'Perhaps he's queer!'

'Oh no, I don't think so!'

Lucasta decided not to mention the art-theft investigations with Hector to either her parents or her sister. At Christmas and from the distance of her father's gloomy vicarage they seemed somehow unreal.

She left the vicarage as soon as she could on the day after Boxing Day and went back to St James's Square on the 28th. She met Hector in the hall as she went in.

'I hope your Christmas was not as bad as you expected!' he said by way of greeting. 'But would you please come into my office. I want to show you something that came in the post this morning.'

Once they were in his office he handed her a bill

which was headed 'Hector Elroy, Art Theft Investigator'. It was addressed to Melvin Delany, Esq., who had sent it back. Across it he had scrawled in charcoal, 'I'm not paying any of this. Thanks to your interference my wife is divorcing me and I shan't have any money.'

'Interference! There's gratitude for you!' said Hector. 'However, let's forget about that one and move on. I'm hopeful that we shall have some successful investigations in the new year, which is nearly upon us. Indeed, a new decade is approaching. I shan't be here for the New Year celebrations as I have to go tomorrow to visit my old mother in the country. I propose that we have a bottle of my father's best champagne together this evening after work. How about it?'

'Hector, I'm sorry,' said Lucasta. 'I've been thinking about it and I've decided not to help you any more with your art theft investigations. I'm going to stick to what you employed me to do – sort out your father's books.'

'But why on earth, Lucasta? I'm sorry if we have encountered a bit of violence, but it will probably never happen again.'

'I'm sorry. I'm not prepared to discuss it. I've made up my mind and that's that!'

After Lucasta had gone, Hector sat gloomily at his desk reading *The Times*, occasionally shaking his head and whistling through his teeth.

'Odd of Lucasta to react like that,' he said to himself. 'Premenstrual tension I expect. She'll probably come round!'

3

January 1970

'How would you like a trip to New York?'

'What for?'

'All free. First class too!'

'I suppose to investigate some theft or other?'

'Absolutely right! This American film star, name of Gloria something-or-other – never heard of her myself – phoned. She's lost a small painting of a cherub. Very upset about it. Wants us to go and investigate.'

'No!'

'Oh, come on please, Lucasta, I may need your help.'

'After our last so-called investigation, as I have told you, I have resolved only to do what I was employed to do – sort out your father's books.'

Hector's face, which had been beaming at the thought of a trip to New York with Lucasta, fell.

'I see. Very well then. I shall have to go on my own. But would you do one small thing for me, please? If anyone telephones Jolly wanting my art-investigating services as opposed to my legal ones, may I ask him to put them on to you? All you have to do is to tell them I'm away on a case in New York. Take the particulars and say we'll deal with it as soon as I get back.'

'*We'll?*'

'Oh, all right. *I'll* deal with it!'

And Hector, still clearly excited by the prospect of New York, left Lucasta to the books in the library. It was coffee-time, she decided, so sat down and poured herself a cup from the flask she brought with her every day. It was black, sweet and strong. She fumbled in her handbag and found the Christmas card she'd received from Duncan in Hong Kong that morning. It was a lurid red colour with an embossed gold pagoda in the middle.

> *Hope this reaches you in time.*
> *All my love and a very Happy Christmas.*

Well, it was a nice thought, even if it was a bit late. She peered at the postmark on the envelope, but there seemed to be no real clue as to when it had been posted.

Five days later, Lucasta was sitting having her morning coffee again thinking about Duncan, and particularly the letter she had received from him that morning, when the telephone on the wall of the library rang and Jolly announced that Mr Hector wished to speak to her and that he was calling from America.

'Look, Lucasta, I've got a problem and you must help me. I traced the stolen picture easily and I'm having a "real great time", as they would put it here, but the picture got damaged and it looks as if there's another painting underneath. Gloria wants me to get an expert to look at it and see what the underpainting is. I haven't a clue who to go to. I thought you might know. . .'

Lucasta sighed. She seemed to be sighing a great deal these days. 'Mm, what date would you give to the cherub picture?'

'It looks – er – old, maybe seventeenth century. Not too sure.'

'Didn't this Gloria tell you who it was by?'

'Well, no signature you see. But a nice little picture.'

'I see.' Lucasta sighed again. 'So, if you are right with your dating, the underpicture will not be later than the 1600s. There is one man in New York I've heard of, but I don't know him. Shall I give you his name? You'll have to look up his address.'

'New York? But we've moved on to LA. Gloria wanted to discuss a film script with a producer. You don't know anyone in LA, I suppose?'

'You do get around, don't you! No, I don't know anyone in LA!'

'Pity. Gloria would like a very quick opinion. She's very excited about it you see.'

'Well I don't know anyone in LA. I do know a man in London though.'

'Can I sell him to Gloria as the *real* expert?'

'I'm sure you can.'

So Lucasta gave his name and address.

'Excellent!' said Hector. 'I'll let you know what she says. I suppose I could bring the picture back with me – it's only very small.'

'You might. I think there may be difficulties at the airport, though, if they find it in your luggage.'

'Well, we'll see. Anyhow, I may not be back for a few days. Jolly says there's nothing urgent and I assume you've had no enquiries. I'm rather enjoying myself as a matter of fact. I'm promised a tour of a film studio tomorrow.'

Lucasta sighed again. 'Well, have a good time. I'll still be here when you get back I expect.'

Lucasta put the phone back on its rest and went and sat down. She had that morning discovered three large cupboards at the end of the library which she'd not been able to reach before because of the books stacked on the floor in front of them. Each of the cupboards was piled high with yet more books. And these books seemed to be the most valuable. Some of them were very old and she would have to do some research before she sold them. And then in her handbag was the letter from Duncan. She knew the contents by heart.

> *Dearest Lucasta, I'm sorry to have to write you this letter. One of the girls working with me on the project is Wang Li. She's a very lovely person and I'm sure you'd like her if you met her. In the run-up to Christmas and over the holiday we have become 'very close' as they say. In the circumstances, if you want to call off our engagement I shall fully understand. I wanted to be honest with you. Duncan. I still love you.*

Lucasta always took her engagement ring off while sorting the books. Now she took the small box in which she kept it out of the zip-up compartment in her handbag and looked at the ring. It was a single large diamond and she remembered how pleased she'd been when Duncan had given it to her. But as she looked at it in its little velvet-lined box, a strange feeling of suffocation came over her. She really couldn't stay in the library any longer. She took off her plastic hat and put her big overcoat over her boiler suit and ran down the stairs and out into the square. The gardens in the middle were for once unlocked. Although it was freezing cold, she went into them and sat on a bench and breathed in the cold air deeply. She gradually felt better. Then she realised that she was still holding the box with the ring in it.

'Bah!' she said. 'Let him rot in Hong Kong!' And she hurled the box into the litter bin beside the seat. She felt even better after doing that and five minutes later was walking purposefully back up Hector's front steps. A man strangely dressed in an old green duffle coat and wearing a battered brown trilby hat was standing in the hall.

'Ah,' he said as Lucasta came through the door. 'I rang the bell but nobody seemed to be about. . . Good Lord, it's Lucasta, isn't it?'

Then he took off his hat to reveal his prematurely bald head with long whiffs of red hair over his ears and down his neck.

'Derek! I haven't seen you for ages, but you're just as scruffy as ever. How's the art dealing going?'

'Very slow at the moment. As far as I'm concerned there's been a recession on ever since I started dealing three years ago! But how are you? Waspish and lovely as ever, I see. And what are you doing here?'

'I have a temporary job.'

'Painting murals?'

'Don't be stupid, Derek. If you really must know, sorting out some books. And what are you doing here?'

'Hoping to see a chap called Hector Elroy.'

'What about?'

'Oh, just a problem I have.'

'About a picture?'

'Er, yes.'

'Where did you get his name from?'

'I saw an advert.'

43

'It's unbelievable!' said Lucasta.

'Why is it unbelievable?'

'Ah well, never mind,' said Lucasta, sighing. 'Anyhow, you can't see Hector at the moment as he's in New York and Los Angeles hunting for missing pictures.'

'I gather he's a solicitor, too. How on earth does he find time for it all?'

'Oh, he's a very brilliant man!' replied Lucasta without any hint of irony in her voice. 'But I have been known to help him a bit – sometimes.'

'Well look, could you maybe come over to my flat so I can give you more details about the problem?'

'Um, well, I suppose so, yes, seeing as we're old friends and provided it's not too far away.'

Silently Lucasta thought that at least it would be a break from the dusty books and would take her mind off Duncan's letter.

'My flat's in Pimlico and my car's parked out there in the square.'

'Okay. I'll just tell Hector's clerk where I'm going.'

It was only after Lucasta had divested herself of her boiler suit, had had a quick wash and had put on her skirt and jumper, and after Derek had mentioned that the picture in question was probably worth a lot of money, that it dawned on her that she had been foolish in throwing away her engagement ring. Duncan had told her that she ought to insure it as it had cost quite a bit. Of course she hadn't and it had probably cost hundreds and it belonged to her – so she ought to have hung on to it, she now realised. They were seated in Derek's dilapidated sports car by the time she came to the decision that she must retrieve her ring from the litter bin.

'Derek, wait here – or better still, come and help me. I know that it sounds silly, but I've thrown my engagement ring into a litter bin in the gardens and I think I was stupid. Because, like your picture, it's probably worth a lot of money!'

'I'll help of course! Oh Lord – here comes a traffic warden and I'm running out of time. I'll have to talk to him. You go on. Which side of the gardens?'

'The litter bin by the seat in the corner over there.'

But as Lucasta entered the gardens, her heart started pounding. She could see a workman emptying the litter bins into a litter barrow. She raced to the bin by the seat. Empty! She ran over to the workman and his barrow.

'Excuse me, but I put something in that bin over there which I shouldn't have done. Could you please look in your barrow and try and find it?'

'Sorry luv, against regulations.'

'But it's a ring. Rather valuable.'

'Well you'll never find a ring in this lot. Twenty-five bins in here already!'

'But please, I must!'

'Never find it, luv.'

'But it's in a box.'

'Big box?'

'No, a ring box.'

'Very difficult.'

By this time the workman had rolled and lit a cigarette and Derek was approaching.

'Derek, could you please talk to this gentleman? He's emptied the bin I put the ring in and all the rubbish is in his barrow and he says we'll never find it!'

'Well we could try.'

'No, never do it mate,' said the workman. 'Anyhow, legally, all the rubbish belongs to the Council now.'

45

'Er, look old chap,' said Derek in his best public school manner. 'Why don't you take this (he handed him a £5 note) and go and sit over there on that bench and have a quiet smoke, while I and this young lady have a hunt for it. There'll be another of those for you if we find it!'

'Yeah, okay then. I'll take me break now and turn a blind eye. But if I see the supervisor coming round, I'll whistle and you'll have to scarper quick.'

Fortunately, the rubbish barrow consisted of a series of removable metal sections which, with a great deal of heaving, Derek and Lucasta managed to lift out. There were five altogether and they turned each one onto the tarmac path and went through them. Lucasta was amazed at what people put in litter bins in the middle of winter. It was totally disgusting. The most bizarre thing of all was a set of false teeth. But no ring.

'Leave it all there till we've finished,' said Derek. 'If we come to the end and haven't found it, we must have missed it and will have to go through everything again.'

They found the ring in the last container. It occurred to Lucasta as they found it, and as she looked on the diamond once more, that they could have saved a lot of time if they'd asked the workman if he'd any idea into which container he'd emptied the corner bin. But you never thought of things like that when you were in a panic! She showed the ring to Derek and was pocketing it when she heard a shrill whistling. She looked towards the workman who had risen from his bench and was gesticulating at them furiously.

'Better go!'

'What about putting the rubbish back?'

'Don't know. Must go I think.'

And so they scarpered into Derek's car and drove off with a great revving and roaring.

'Pity you couldn't give him the other £5!'

'Yes, still it saved you a bit. You only owe me £5 now,' remarked Derek with some satisfaction.

Lucasta had always remembered Derek as a 'messy' sort of person when she was on the art course with him. But she was unprepared for the state of his flat in Pimlico. It was at the top of a period house and the hall and stairs were quite well kept. But once they were inside the flat, the chaos was indescribable. An old bicycle was propped up against the wall by the front door. *'Quite an athletic feat to carry it up all those stairs,'* thought Lucasta. They threaded their way through an enormous number of grubby black dustbin bags from which rubbish spilled in all directions, and past a pile of dirty washing and a heap of old magazines, as Derek led her to a clearer part of the living room. The walls here were covered with pictures, mainly modern. Derek indicated an abstract which Lucasta recognised as being by a very well-known artist. It consisted of three yellow blobs on a bright magenta background.

'Look at it!' said Derek, lowering his voice. 'I think something's wrong with it. Have a careful look . . . Sorry, I must check to see if Anita's in before we go any further. . . . Anita! Are you there?' he bellowed down a passage which presumably led to the bedrooms. He then disappeared for a minute and came back smiling. 'She's out,' he said, 'so we can discuss this openly.'

'And who, may I ask, is Anita? And personally I would like to have a good wash before we go any further after sorting through all that rubbish.'

'Of course. We both should wash. Bathroom down there, second on left. I'll do myself at the kitchen sink. Anita is my ex-wife. She lives here in the spare bedroom and that's her easel over there. She paints.'

'Your ex-wife? Living in the spare bedroom? A bit unusual, isn't it?'

'She's nowhere else to go. I'll explain after we've washed.'

The bathroom was as messy as the rest of the flat, but Lucasta had a good wash of her hands and arms and face in the grubby basin in cold water, as there didn't seem to be any hot, and dried them on an old towelling dressing gown hanging behind the door, as there didn't seem to be any towels. She then joined Derek in the sitting room and they looked at the picture together.

'You see, I think Anita may have copied it and sold the original.'

'Why do you think that?'

Derek grew quite heated.

'She keeps telling me I'm a mean old bugger and should give her more money. Well, it's unfair, given how she behaved, and seeing as how I'm putting her up in the spare room *and* letting her paint here. And all after I bought out her share in the flat!'

'Why do you think that's not the original?'

'Well, it looks funny somehow. . .'

'If she copied it, wouldn't there be signs of interference with the pins holding it in the frame?'

'Mm. I've looked. I can't see any. But you see, she'd have been very careful, wouldn't she, in picking out the pins and putting them back in the same place?'

Lucasta took down the picture. It was an oil painted on hardboard. The frame was very simple – of plain pine. She could see no interference with the frame or the picture at all and so she put the picture back on the wall.

'Anyone else been in the flat recently that you know of?'

'No, I don't think so. Only the cleaner. She comes in once a week to tidy up. As you can probably tell, she's due tomorrow. Wonderful woman. Black as coal. She cleans the place up beautifully, and then of course we mess it up again as soon as she's gone!'

'And do you do your dealing from here?'

'Ah, yes, but nobody's been in the last week. I told you, trade is very slow.'

'And what about Anita? Would she have had any friends to visit? . . .' Lucasta suddenly stopped. She realised she was sounding like Hector when he was investigating. And what was she doing here anyway? She'd said she wouldn't help any more. But Derek, for all his oddities, had been a good friend in the past . . . 'Well, we'll see what Hector has to say when he gets back. I can't take it any further at the minute, I'm afraid.'

'Well, to answer your question, Anita's become a recluse. She wouldn't have had anyone to visit her. By the way, I'm very sorry to hear about your engagement. Presumably it's off, is it?'

'Yes.'

'Feeling very sore about it?'

'I don't think it's sunk in yet; but somehow I was expecting it.'

'I see. Tell you what – you can treat me to lunch and I won't press you for the £5 I gave to the workman!'

Lucasta agreed. As well as there being no hot water, there didn't appear to be any heating in Derek's flat. She shivered and Derek looked at her.

'I've probably forgotten to pay the gas bill! I'm rather bad at things like that.'

Meanwhile (give or take the time difference), Hector was driving down Sunset Boulevard in a large rented American car. He'd always wanted to drive that sort of thing since he'd seen them in films of the 1940s, and he was very pleased with it. It rolled beautifully and the air conditioning was wonderful. Since arriving in LA he'd been more than a little uncomfortable in his heavy pinstripe suit, though it had been perfectly all right in New York of course. Gloria, when she initially greeted him, had told him that he looked 'just cute' in it, but in LA he felt it was unsuitable. Anyhow, he wasn't stopping for long, so, just as a gesture to LA culture, he'd dispensed with his tie and waistcoat. Although he looked a trifle ludicrous, he also felt extremely happy. His visit to New York had been successful and exciting. Gloria had arranged for him to stay at a very smart hotel at her expense. She had turned out to be what Hector considered a really elegant lady of uncertain age. Possibly nearer fifty than forty. She was tall, blonde, and had very pale white skin. She was both amiable and excitable, and when Hector had traced the whereabouts of the cherub picture so quickly, she had flung her arms about him and hugged him so hard that he'd felt well, let's say indescribable! And then there'd been the business of the picture being damaged and the other picture being visible underneath. But in the middle of all that, Gloria had received a telephone call from the producer in LA and had announced: 'We must all go to Hollywood at once, and you too, Hector darling. You say you've never been to LA and I'm sure you'd love it! We'll change your ticket so you can fly back to

London direct from LA And you *must* have a trip round a movie studio.'

So Hector had joined Gloria's entourage, as he had come to think of it. It consisted of a maid/dresser, a hairdresser/manicurist and a chauffeur. The English manservant had been dismissed over the picture theft . . .

Gloria always travelled in a stretch limo, so she and her entourage were met by one at LA airport, whither they were all transported to her place on Sunset Boulevard. Hector was told he could use one of the innumerable spare bedrooms for a couple of nights. It was a beautiful room – so different from his bedroom in St. James's.

And so Hector smiled as he drove along. Yes, Gloria really was a very lovely lady, even though she did try to make herself out to be years younger than she obviously was when viewed close to. And the business of having an entourage was ridiculous too. The English butler had been sacked – which was a good thing – but the chauffeur was totally effeminate in spite of his bulging muscles (he doubled as a bodyguard) and the maid and the hairdresser seemed to be engaged in some sort of lesbian affair. This appeared to give Gloria great amusement. Anyhow, he'd been able to knock back an enormous quantity of champagne, which was very pleasant, even though some of it was Californian, and now he'd been asked to attend the meeting with the film producer as Gloria's attorney, as her usual one was away somewhere.

'But Gloria, I know nothing about film law, and even less about Californian law,' he'd protested.

'Darling. . . you'll be wonderful. I just want you to protect me from Max. He's a bastard.'

So he was now on his way to Max's suite in a hotel

in Beverly Hills in his hired car trailing behind Gloria's white stretch limo, and after the meeting he was going on for his trip round the film studios. He was a little delayed due to his unfamiliarity with the complexities of 'valet parking', and by the time he was shown in to Max's suite an argument was already in full swing between Max and Gloria. They were standing about ten feet apart, glaring at one another.

'Look, honey, don't take on so. Give me five,' Max was saying. 'I want to make a call.' He grasped a telephone and punched out a number. 'Nymie,' he bellowed, 'I'm waiting to hear from you. You said you'd get me out of this hellhole pronto. I'm still here. What's keeping you?'

Hector heard a muffled response from the other end.

'Well it ain't good enough. I want to be out of here within the next thirty minutes after I've finished with Gloria. Got it? . . . Now, darling, as I was saying: No can do.'

Hector by this time had realised that Max, who was a man in his sixties, bald and fat, was strangely dressed in a pair of blue denim dungarees which he couldn't do up at the side because of his bulging stomach. A diamond glittered in a ring on his finger and he waved a very large cigar about as he spoke.

'What the hell do you mean?'

Gloria looked very angry indeed. Two big red spots had appeared on her normally pale cheeks.

'Like I say, honey, no can do.'

'But you promised me the part!'

'Well I've changed my mind.'

'Who, may I ask, are you going to give it to?'

'Haven't decided yet. But I don't think you look young enough.'

'How dare you, Max! God, I'll sue you. This is my attorney just arrived. I'll sue him, won't I, Hector?'

'Well, I don't know,' stuttered Hector. 'Look, we'd better go into another room and discuss it if, er, Max will allow.'

'Sure, go ahead. You can't sue me darling, there's no contract.'

'My God, I'll kill him,' shrieked Gloria once she and Hector were in an adjoining bedroom. Gone was Gloria's normal poise and calm. She looked mad and Hector realised that as a woman she may have been charming, but as a client she was going to be difficult and emotional. However, rising to his full height and looking down into Gloria's face, he said, 'Just tell me, Gloria, what you and Max agreed about this film. What's it called?'

'*Danger Be My Friend*, of course, and Max said I could play the lead.'

'But were any other terms discussed? How much you were to be paid, that sort of thing.'

'No.'

'Did you put off accepting any other work because of it?'

'Well I could have had a thousand parts, but everyone knew that I was going to do *Danger*.'

'But did anyone actually offer you a part?'

'Er . . . no.'

'Well, as I said, I know nothing about Californian law, but under English law I wouldn't advise you to sue.'

Hector thought he'd never seen anyone look so angry. Gloria didn't look just angry even, she looked like a lunatic.

'You don't know what you're talking about,' she spat at him. 'You're a fool!'

Hector remained very calm.

'Very well – there's a phone by the bed. Call the best movie attorney (he was rather proud of his American phraseology) in LA and see what he says.'

'I shall, and you can wait outside in the hallway!'

'Very well,' said Hector calmly and went into the hall, where he sat on a very uncomfortable upright chair beside a table with an elaborate floral arrangement on it. From there he could hear Max yelling instructions down his telephone in the sitting room of the suite.

After ten minutes or so, the door of the bedroom opened and Gloria reappeared. She seemed quite collected, but stared straight in front of her. Hector got up from his chair.

'Well?' he asked.

Gloria walked straight past him and out of the suite and banged the door behind her.

Hector was not sure if he should say goodbye to Max, but decided against it. When he got outside the hotel he noticed that the sky had suddenly darkened. But he supposed he'd better continue with his visit to the film studios.

'And that was that,' said Derek in the restaurant. 'The first two I overlooked, but coming in with a potential client and finding my wife *in flagrante* on the sofa in the middle of my valuable stock of lovely modern art was too much even for such an easy-going man as me. At least you were told by letter, not by visual display!'

'You poor thing!' said Lucasta, patting Derek's hand. The lunch was going to cost her very much more than £5.

'You're very sympathetic, Lucasta. Come back to the flat. I've got some very good Turkish coffee to sober us up a bit. I'll nick the fan heater from Anita's bedroom.'

The coffee was indeed very good, but its sobering effect was ruined by a bottle of Calvados which Derek found in the kitchen cupboard.

'You know I came across Melv recently, who taught us figure drawing,' said Lucasta by way of conversation.

'Ah yes, old Melv! How was he?'

'Somewhat lecherous!'

'Yes, he always was I think. But the sight of you would be enough to make anyone lecherous. You know I've always liked you, Lucasta. You're so attractive. Lovely figure, lovely legs. That mini-skirt more or less reveals all, doesn't it? In fact, I'd rather look at your legs than my lovely pictures at the moment. Can I come over and sit on the floor beside you?'

And without waiting for her reply, that's what he did.

Lucasta, who had only had one glass of Calvados, was pleased that someone, even if it was only Derek, seemed to like her. She was feeling very rejected. But when he put his bald head on her lap and groaned slightly she thought it was time to take evasive action. She'd been sitting in an armchair opposite the picture Derek thought looked strange and an idea had occurred to her – no doubt helped by the Calvados.

'Excuse me one moment, Derek, please,' she said, gently pushing his head off her skirt. 'I want to have another look at that picture.'

She went over and took it off the wall, then looked at the picture cord that was holding it up.

'Just as I thought,' she cried triumphantly. 'It's been

hung upside down. I can tell from the way the cord is marked. How's that?' she said, re-hanging the picture.

Derek scrambled to his feet. As he stood beside her swaying slightly and clutching his glass he said, 'Goodness, I do believe you're right! That bloody cleaning woman must have taken it down to dust it and put it back wrongly. Lucasta, you're wonderful! Here, I must kiss you.'

Lucasta was glad to escape from the ensuing tussle with all her clothes still more or less on. She grabbed her coat and handbag and fled down the stairs.

'Well, good trip?' asked Lucasta as Hector entered the library two days later.

'Quite successful in some ways. Got terrible jetlag though. I think Jolly said you'd had an enquiry while I was away.'

'Oh, that's right. I've written you a little note all about it – it's on your desk somewhere. It was for an old friend of mine and I dealt with it. I don't think you can make a charge for what I did, though. Also, I'm afraid I shall be here somewhat longer than I thought. I discovered that those two cupboards at the end there are crammed with books too. Some of them look rare and old.'

'Good Lord! Do you think they'll be worth a lot?'

'I can't really tell. I must do some research.'

'Well, I'm jolly glad you're not leaving yet anyhow.'

'Did you know that Duncan's broken off our engagement?'

'Good Lord, no! When did this happen?'

'While you were away. He found some Chinese girl.'

'I *am* sorry, Lucasta. I wouldn't have thought it of Duncan. Known him years. Steady sort of chap, I always thought. Still, I know that these Chinese girls can be terribly attractive.'

'Well thank you, Hector! Meaning I suppose that I'm not!'

'No, no, no. I didn't mean it like that. No, I've always thought you were – er – well – most attractive!'

'Well, you've never mentioned it before.'

'Of course not. One doesn't say that sort of thing to a friend's fiancée.'

'I see.'

Lucasta seemed somewhat mollified, Hector thought. Although she did look rather odd in her boiler suit with a plastic shower cap on her head.

'In fact,' he continued, 'you even look quite attractive dressed like that. Look, I'd like you to come with me to take the picture of the cherub to that fellow you told me about. He's only a few streets away. And then, if you like, I'll take you out to lunch at Scott's, as I'm sure you want to hear all about my trip to the States!'

'Oh, all right, I suppose so,' said Lucasta, taking off her plastic shower cap.

Five minutes later Lucasta was in Hector's office looking at the cherub painting and the damage thereto.

'Mm, what's underneath looks quite interesting, but the cherub's not bad. You never told me who stole it or how it got damaged, though.'

'Thought you were never going to ask me that,' said Hector enthusiastically. 'Hilarious really. This film star named Gloria – nice-looking woman, but a bit mutton dressed up as lamb – lives in an apartment, as they call it, in Manhattan. Large place – has to be because she has a large resident entourage, as I called it. She had an English butler chap who was really creepy. Not a nice fellow. Black jacket, pinstripe trousers, silver hair, thin as a rake. Kept on telling me about all the titled people he'd worked for. And there was a chauffeur; great big muscular fellow, but a real pansy.'

'Hector, do you mean he was a homosexual?'

'May have been. I didn't find out, but he was as I say a real pansy . . . Kept rolling his eyes and flexing his muscles. Doubled as Gloria's bodyguard. And then there was a maid-cum-dresser and a hairdresser-manicurist. Now they seem to be having some sort of quite open heavy lesbian affair, which Gloria condoned. She seemed to think it very amusing.'

'A remarkable apartment, you could say. Anyhow, who'd stolen the cherub?'

'Well, it was easy. I questioned them all of course. Before it disappeared one night, the cherub hung over the dining-room fireplace. Artificial fire, of course. Cherub, I thought, aha! As you see, he's got a nice little chubby bottom. I asked all the women if they'd ever seen either of the men or any male visitor looking, well, longingly at the picture. Well, they all said the same. William – that's the creepy manservant – had a sort of fixation on the picture and was always staring at it. So, as it happened to be his half day the next day, I searched his room, with Gloria's permission of course, and there I found it under a pile of underwear in his chest of drawers, along with several *very* pornographic magazines. Well, to say that Gloria was pleased would be an understatement. Of course the silly fellow has damaged the paintwork, as you see – there and there. God knows what masturbation fantasy he was going through at the time!'

Lucasta was silent for several moments and sat looking primly at the damage to the picture. Then she couldn't help laughing.

They dropped the cherub off at the expert's gallery.

The great man was away abroad, but a member of his staff promised that he would look at the picture on his return.

In recounting his adventures further over lunch at Scott's, Hector rather glossed over his muted departure from Gloria, who had never spoken to him again, but who had sent her hairdresser to his bedroom with a message to say that she was still too upset to talk to him, but that she would like to know about the picture, and here was his fee, and his changed air tickets would be with the travel agent.

4

February 1970

As Hector and Lucasta returned from Scott's and entered the hall outside Hector's office, they were greeted by Jolly, who seemed in a state of great agitation. He was wringing his hands together and hopping miserably from foot to foot.

'Mrs Elroy, your mother, sir. She's been on the telephone five times. She seems most upset, sir. It's something to do with her church I think – a theft. But I can't quite make it out. I said I would ask you to telephone her as soon as you returned.'

Lucasta noticed a change come over Hector as Jolly was speaking. At first he looked horrified and then gradually he drew himself up to his full and not inconsiderable height, and stuck out his chin and then his chest.

'Thank you, Jolly. I will deal with it. Five times, you say she's telephoned?'

'Yes sir, five. I kept a careful note.'

'For goodness' sake! Come into my office with me please, Lucasta. I need moral support.'

'Why? What's the matter?'

'My mother is very difficult, if not impossible. Please sit down over there and smile at me from time to time while I'm on the phone.' As he was saying this, he was dialling a number and standing very straight behind his desk.

'Hello Mother. I've only just come back in . . . Well . . . how could I know that you'd want me? Now what's the matter? Jolly said something had been stolen from the church . . . The altar? How could anyone steal the altar? . . . Oh yes, of course, it's a wooden communion table, isn't it? . . . Someone just came in and took it? . . . Yes, I see!'

There was then a lengthy tirade down the telephone from the other end, which Lucasta could hear from where she was sitting several yards away.

'Yes, yes, yes, now calm down, Mother! Yes, of course, I'll come down straight away, but please try to calm yourself. Have you spoken to the vicar?'

This last remark occasioned a further tirade.

'Look, Mother, you're wasting time, I can't come straight away if you keep talking, can I?'

Apparently this satisfied Mrs Elroy and Hector put the receiver down and sank into his desk chair.

'Please, please, Lucasta, come with me to see my mother. She's in a terrible state, as you will have gathered. Somebody's stolen the communion table – it's Elizabethan – from her church and she somehow thinks I can get it back for her – "Just like that", as Tommy Cooper says. It will be totally traumatic, but I'm sure you'll be able to calm her down a bit.'

'How do you know?'

'One just gets, well, hunches about these things.'

'It doesn't sound as if it is going to be very easy, from what I've just heard coming down the phone. Why is she like that?'

'She's always been like it. Why do you think my father came to live here?'

'Oh, okay,' said Lucasta, and she was soon sitting beside Hector in his car.

'At this rate I'll never get any legal work done! There were quite a few things waiting for me when I came back from the States – nothing vitally urgent, but one can't leave things for ever. Look, Lucasta, it's terribly kind of you to come with me. I really do appreciate it, you know!'

'Well, yes. But you'd better tell me all about your family so that I know what to expect.'

'Well, Mother didn't have me until she was 45 or so. I was quite a shock as she and the old man had been married, as far as I can gather, in perfect marital disharmony for twenty years. They lived in Pinner then, in a largish villa. Father used to travel to the City every day on the Metropolitan line along with hundreds of other City gents wearing bowlers, carrying briefcases and rolled umbrellas, and with copies of *The Times* under their arms. I can just remember the old house. I liked it. Then, when I was about five, Mother inherited this large estate in Hampshire from her uncle – her father's brother. He had no children and my mother was an only child. So we all moved there. It's in some ways a wonderful place, as you will see, but I have never really liked it, I suppose because I was never happy there. We inherited three servants from my great-uncle, who lived on his own there, but by then they were getting rather old. I had to have a full-time nanny, befitting my new social station, although why a boy of five needs a nanny I don't know! Father was supposed to give up his partnership in his firm and stay at home and be the local squire, and Mother took on the role of Lady Bountiful in the village and the district around it.'

'Ah! I thought you must have had a nanny.'

'Why?'

'Never mind at the moment. I'll explain later. Go on.'

'Well, Father got fed up with his new role after about a year or so and moved here, where he set up in practice. He used to come home once a fortnight on a Saturday afternoon, stay for the night, and depart again after lunch on Sunday. He always claimed to be very, very busy, you see. As far as I know, he never had any other women, but of course he may have done. He was a very quiet and discreet person. I was sent away to school when I was eight, and that was pretty grim, but I frankly dreaded coming home for the holidays. Mother, by this time, had engaged a young-ish couple to look after her and they've remained faithfully with her, although they must be past retirement age by now. How people put up with her I don't know. I once asked them. "Practice, Mr Hector," was all that I could get out of Jenkins. As you'll see, there's this sodding great house with the parish church quite literally beside its rear lawn and a large park and a home farm, which Mother let against my father's advice some years ago. There's a small village with a pub and a post office and general store. There are several estate cottages, some of which have been let out as weekend homes. Credit where credit's due, though – Mother has never sold anything.'

'I see. Your mother must be very old then?'

'Yes. She's over ninety. Though you would never know it physically. She lives in a time warp.'

'As your father did!'

'I suppose so, yes. Nothing has changed in the house since I was a boy. I think that the Jenkinses must have bought the fridge and the washing machine with their own money. Mother never goes into the kitchen and has nothing to do with the shopping.'

'Well,' said Lucasta, 'I look forward to seeing all this. You seemed to be worried about money when we were in Norfolk, but presumably you will inherit the estate from your mother.'

'Mother owns it outright and she's no intention of passing anything over to me until time has taken its course. There'll be a huge amount of death duty to pay, so undoubtedly I shall have to sell the whole lot. Although I had been earning a great deal when I worked for the firm in Lincoln's Inn, now I have just a small private income, and Father's practice just about breaks even. That's why I'm hoping some of the books may be valuable and, well, I'll be frank, it's why I'm advertising my services as an investigator of art thefts.'

'Yes, I know that.'

'Oh! How?'

'Someone told me – they were connected with the enquiry you had here while you were in the States.'

'I see!'

Hector looked so crestfallen that Lucasta wanted to pat his hand as she had done with Derek, but somehow she thought she'd better not.

'There we are,' said Hector some time later. 'Long Wensum.'

'Ah – yes, I see what you mean,' said Lucasta.

The house with its church and parkland were impressive and unspoilt but somehow dismal and lacking in charm.

A grey-haired gentleman in black trousers and a grey jacket opened the door to them. *He must be Jenkins*, thought Lucasta.

'Pleasant to see you, sir, in spite of the tragic circumstances. Mrs Elroy's in the drawing room.'

Jenkins led Hector, with Lucasta following behind,

down a long hallway and through double doors into a large room with three full-length windows which over-looked the lawn and the church.

'And about time too, Hector. You don't know how worried I've been. It's absolutely disgraceful. It's theft and it's blasphemy all at once. I wouldn't have believed it! It's impossible.'

'Yes Mother. Try to calm down. Just tell me – when did it go missing? I mean, who noticed it was gone?'

Lucasta, who was standing in the background, noticed that Hector's usual calm composure was gone. And how on earth could such a tiny, thin woman as Mrs Elroy was produce such a large son as Hector?

'Lunchtime, of course. That's why I was ringing you all afternoon. Lunchtime. That silly woman who does the flowers came rushing across the lawn, apparently – told Jenkins that the altar was missing. He wouldn't believe her of course, but then she got him to have a look and he reported it to me.'

'And have you been over and had a look yourself?'

'Of course not – what, at my age?'

'But Mother, you go across to church every Sunday. . .'

'That's different. No, I trust Jenkins' word abso-lutely!'

'It's Friday today isn't it?'

'Of course it is. Don't you even know what day of the week it is now?'

'Well, generally yes, Mother, but you see I've been in the United States and you get a trifle confused with the time changes and that sort of thing.'

'The United States! That's America isn't it? I sup-pose it was for one of your art-theft capers that you told me about. Your father never had to go abroad all the time he was practising law.'

'Well yes, it was about an art theft, Mother.'

'Good. So now you can get to work on finding the stolen altar. I know why they stole it. That stupid young vicar – the one before this one – unscrewed it from the wall and moved it forward so he could say Communion facing us all. Some new-fangled idea from Rome. Ridiculous! He was a very ugly fellow too. It wouldn't have been so bad if he'd been handsome like Mr Miller – you remember him in the fifties? A very nice man – but he – I can't remember his name – was very ugly and had a big red nose. He didn't stay long though, thank goodness. But this new one is not much better and has still insisted on facing us all. Thieves couldn't have stolen the table if it had been still screwed to the wall. No, they would have needed a screwdriver and it would have taken ages and they'd have been caught. As it was, they just lifted it and marched off with it. At least the candlesticks and the cross were put away somewhere or else they would have had them too, no doubt. I've telephoned the Bishop but he's not answering.'

Mrs Elroy paused for breath, her small chest quivering under her pearls and twin-set. It was getting dark in the room and she peered bad-temperedly through the gloom to where Lucasta was standing.

'And who's that over there?' she asked Hector.

'Oh, that's my friend Lucasta,' replied Hector.

'Gosh!' thought Lucasta. 'I've been elevated from "assistant" to "friend"!'

After considerable argument, Hector managed to persuade his mother that he really couldn't do much investigating that day as it was now getting dark. But to pacify her, he and Lucasta did make their way to the church and, with the aid of a torch, examined the ground outside the doorway. As Mrs Elroy was a patron of the living, she had her own personal key to the church, which they now used to open the main door and go in, switching on the lights in order to have a look round. The church itself, Lucasta noted, was totally unremarkable. Small and unadorned, it had no special features apart from, presumably, the Elizabethan communion table which, before it was stolen, had stood away from the east wall in the middle of the sanctuary. Hector could see the marks of the four feet where it had stood, and on careful examination, he could also make out where it had originally been fastened to the east wall by means of four brackets. The screw holes had only been filled in roughly.

'Mmm,' said Hector. 'Dreary church, isn't it? Just like the rest of the place. Can't do much more today I think. I suppose we shall have to stay the night.'

'But Hector, I haven't brought any things with me – toothbrush, hairbrush, pyjamas. . .'

'Nor clean underwear. No, nor have I, just like when we took the statue to Scotland. We'll just have to manage. Mother will give us beds and we can get some sort of a meal at the pub, I hope. I don't suppose the Jenkinses were expecting us for dinner.'

But as it turned out, Hector was wrong.

'I've told Mrs Jenkins you'll be stopping to dinner and I've asked her to air the beds in two single rooms, whatever your private sleeping arrangements are,' Mrs Elroy announced on their return, glaring belligerently collectively and individually at Hector and Lucasta. 'I won't have that sort of thing under my roof!'

'"That sort of thing", as you call it, is not taking place, I assure you, Mother. Lucasta has in fact been employed by me to sort out Father's library. She's also ably assisted me on one or two of my investigations. That is why I asked her to come with me.'

Lucasta didn't think anyone actually said it and that it was only printed in books, but Mrs Elroy did actually utter 'Harrumph!' 'Well, I shall open some wine. It's nice to have you for dinner, Hector – you usually only come for Sunday lunch. Do you like wine, Lucasta?'

'Yes, thank you.'

'Good. Come a bit closer so I can see you properly. My eyesight is not as good as it used to be.'

This is awful! thought Lucasta. *But I'd better not antagonise her.* And so she stepped two or three paces forward, conscious that she was dressed very plainly in a green jumper and grey trousers. There was a long silence as Mrs Elroy looked her up and down.

'Mmm . . . Not bad looking at all. You've got a very large bust, haven't you? I don't suppose you can see your feet if you look down!'

For a moment Lucasta felt as though she should look down to see if it were true. She'd never thought of it before – but she restrained herself.

'Yes. You'll do!' said Mrs Elroy enigmatically. 'Now Hector, draw up a chair for Lucasta. Why are you letting her stand all this time? I shall ring for some sherry!'

In the morning, Hector and Lucasta had another look at the church, together with the graveyard and surrounding area.

'We'd better go and talk to the vicar, I suppose,' said Hector. 'But I can't see us getting far with this one!'

The night had not been too bad. Spring was

coming, but it was still cold. Lucasta had had a stone hot water bottle in her bed and Mrs Jenkins had lent her a very warm nightie. She wished she didn't keep having dreams about Duncan kissing a very small and pretty Chinese girl. In the morning, gritting her teeth, she resolved that she must forget all about him. Other men seemed to like her. She thought of Grimes and Derek and Melvin. But that was not really the sort of thing she wanted. Anyhow, she would force herself to be cheerful!

Hector had been given a disposable razor to shave with and there had been, amazingly, plenty of hot water, given that the plumbing looked as though it dated from the nineteenth century.

The new vicarage that housed the present vicar was in a nearby village called Dimmer, the original vicarage near the church having been sold off by the Church Commissioners to a stockbroker.

Although they'd been given directions to it by Jenkins, it proved difficult to locate. Hector had been looking for at least a substantial house, but it turned out to be a small bungalow with an overgrown front garden. But it was definitely the vicarage, because it said so on a notice on the front gate.

The door was opened slowly by a young man in jeans and a pullover. He was bare-footed and was holding a guitar.

'I suppose you know it's my day off,' he said by way of a welcome.

'Well, I'm sorry, no, we didn't. My name's Hector Elroy – and you are the vicar, I presume? The communion table has been stolen from the church near my mother's house.'

'Oh yes – I see why you're here now. Well, you'd better both come in. Have a seat.'

He twanged a chord on his guitar and reluctantly propped it against the wall.

'My mother, as you know, is elderly, and has asked me to help her. May I ask you a few questions?'

'Fire away. My name's Jim, by the way. Smoke? No? Very wise.'

Jim lit a cigarette and dropped the match nonchalantly into the already full ashtray beside his armchair.

'Well, first, have the police been informed?' asked Hector.

'Yes.'

'Are they doing anything?'

'No, I don't think so. There's been a spate of thefts from churches in the area. That's why I keep all mine locked – that is, apart from the one near your mother, which she seems to regard as her own private chapel. She gets her manservant to open it every day. I never bother to bring my own key when I take services there.'

'I see!' said Hector, glancing knowingly at Lucasta. 'Have the church authorities been told about the theft?'

'I left a message for the rural dean, but he hasn't called back yet. You see, we're all desperately overworked. I've got six churches to look after. It's impossible!!'

'Is the communion table insured, do you know?'

'Couldn't really tell you at the moment. Probably not.'

'It used to be fixed to the wall, I believe. Being freestanding facilitated its removal.'

'Yes. My predecessor moved it so he could face the congregation, and then he left about six months ago. Nobody stays here very long.'

'Well, my mother says – and it seems to me quite

rightly – that one can't have a church, at least not an Anglican church, without an altar. What are you going to do?'

'Oh, I expect we'll rig something up temporarily. There are some old trestle tables in the parish room here. We could use one of those – cover it with a piece of cloth.'

'Will you be able to do that by tomorrow?'

'Shouldn't think so – at least, not unless somebody else organises it!' said Jim, drawing heavily on his cigarette. 'As I said, it's my day off.'

'Well, you wouldn't mind if we organised it? A communion service is scheduled for eight tomorrow morning, I believe.'

'Yes, I think that's right. Let me look at my list.'

Jim languidly rummaged among a pile of papers on a low coffee table beside his chair.

'Yes, you're right,' he said, passing the list to Hector, who found it incomprehensible as it contained service times for six churches for a whole month, as well as the names of who was to read and who was to take the collection; several names had been scored out in various colours of ink and there were sundry arrows indicating the swapping of services, churches and readers.

'I see,' said Hector. 'Well, I'll try and arrange it, but I expect the trestles are rather big to go in my car. Is there any other way of taking one to Long Wensum from here?'

'You could try the farmer in Longie, as I call it; he's been a church warden in the past and he must have a tractor and trailer. Your mother must know his number. Ah, no! Now I remember, they're not speaking. Fell out over something!'

'Got any other farmers who might be helpful?'

'Don't know. They're a miserable and unhelpful lot, farmers in general, as you probably know.'

'Er . . . yes. I'll ask Jenkins, he may be able to help – but I suppose one could use any table from my mother's house, suitably draped?'

'Sure. I'll leave it to you. Ring me if you can't organise something. Now, if you'll excuse me, I must get on with my guitar practice.'

This thought seemed to animate him considerably as he showed them out.

'There's a nice side table in the drawing room which I'm sure would work a treat,' said Lucasta, 'with a white sheet shoved over it.'

'Um, I suppose so. You vicars' daughters are very matter-of-fact about this sort of thing, aren't you?'

'I didn't know you were at all religious.'

'I'm not really – but I do think things should be done properly in church. Anyhow, it would appear we cannot rely on any help at the moment from either the church or the police. Mother will go mad when I tell her! What on earth can I do? She'll go on and on and on and on and on. You've seen and heard her!'

'Let me think,' said Lucasta. 'But first could we please drive to the nearest town so we can buy a few things?'

'That table over there draped with a white sheet! I never heard the like – it's disgraceful! You say this was Lucasta's idea?'

'Yes, Mother. Her father's a vicar you see.'

'Missionaries in the jungle and places like that have to make do with anything, I've been told,' responded Lucasta boldly, recalling her father's very boring reminiscences about when he'd been a young missionary.

'Well, our vicar's not a missionary and we're not in

the jungle!' retorted Mrs Elroy. 'I refuse to take part in such a charade. You'll have to tell the vicar to cancel our service and we'll come to the one they have at nine o'clock in Spelling. You can drive me in your car, Hector. I'll get Jenkins to phone the others who usually come to my church. Get on the phone to the vicar at once, Hector, and tell him.'

Hector did as commanded, but no one at the vicarage answered the phone.

'I suppose I could go and see him again to make sure it all goes ahead. He's obviously not answering his phone as it's his day off,' he said to Lucasta.

'I shouldn't bother. He couldn't be bothered with us. He's probably finished his guitar practice and gone out somewhere. Anyhow, I have premonitions of a fiasco.'

'If anything goes wrong, Mother's sure to blame me.'

'No she won't, because you won't be here. I'm going to go out now and telephone you from the call box in the village, disguising my voice for Jenkins' benefit as he takes all the calls. I shall tell you that you must come back to the office at once as something urgent has occurred. That way you'll miss the likely shambles over tomorrow's service and you won't have to listen to your mother complaining about it. It will also give you Sunday to catch up with all those pressing legal problems you say you have. Then on Monday I suggest you start hunting for another communion table as soon as possible.'

'But how on earth do I do that?'

'There must be several dealers who specialise in church furnishing. They'll be in a book called *The Antique Dealers of England* or something – there's sure to be a copy in your club library. Ring round, visit a few – use your initiative! I cannot see anything other than an exact replacement satisfying your mamma. When you get it here, we must have it fixed to the wall very securely, in spite of any protests from the vicar.'

Hector listened to Lucasta with growing amazement.

'Of course you're absolutely right. How very clever. But it seems a bit of a tall order to get another communion table exactly like the old one. Anyhow, I'll try. And what are you going to be doing while I'm using my initiative, as you call it?'

'I shall stay with your mother and keep her calm, otherwise she'll keep phoning you and you'll never get anything done or any peace!'

'Good Lord! Will you, Lucasta? How on earth will you deal with her?'

'You'll see!'

It was the following Thursday when Hector telephoned Lucasta with encouraging news.

'Look, are you alone? Yes, good – well you won't believe this, but I've found the very thing! I took the measurements from the feet marks on the carpet, as you suggested before I left, and these match almost exactly. And as for the table itself, well, it looks very similar, as far as I remember the original. Never took much notice in fact.'

'Very good indeed! Where did you find it?'

'I've been all over London during the past few days and I went to see a dealer this morning in one of those antique centres who said he thought he might have something suitable. However, when I saw it, it was no good at all, like all the others I'd seen. I was wandering out of the centre when I saw this table standing outside one of the shops. It had obviously just been delivered. So I approached the owner, a rather shady sort of chap in jeans and a leather jacket – hadn't shaved for several days. To cut a long story short, he said the price was four hundred pounds. "Genuine oak and Elizabethan probably, look at the lovely carving." Anyhow, I beat him down to three hundred and fifty pounds, cash . . . had to go to the bank to get it, of course, out of my office account. So, the communion table's on its way and should be delivered tomorrow, Friday afternoon. I hope Mother will be pleased. How have you been getting on, by the way?'

'Splendidly!'

'Good Lord! Really?'

'Really, yes.'

'Can you organise someone to fasten this new table to the east wall?'

'I think Jenkins will be able to do it.'

'Excellent. I'll be down myself, then, tomorrow afternoon in the car.'

By chance, Hector arrived at the same time as the table was being delivered. Jenkins was standing in the chancel with a green apron on instead of his grey coat, fiddling with an electric drill in anticipation. Lucasta was giving the removal men directions.

'Jenkins is very excited about it all, as you can see,' she said to Hector. He's even found the original angle brackets which held the old table to the wall. They were in a box of oddments in the vestry.'

'I'm still a bit worried about the young vicar not liking the altar being fixed back against the wall!' Hector admitted.

'I shouldn't worry too much about him, after last Sunday.'

'What happened?'

'I'll tell you later. That's right – against the wall . . . Thank you. Are you going to be able to move it away enough to fix the brackets, Mr Jenkins?'

'I'm sure we'll manage, miss, seeing that there will be three of us. But if the men could leave the back legs away a bit this side so I can line up the brackets, I'd be grateful . . . I must say, Mr Hector, it's a wonderful match. You'd almost think it was the same table. Miss Lucasta said you bought it from a dealer.'

'Yes, that's right,' said Hector. 'I'm glad you think it's a good match. We'll let you get on with your bracket fixing. Just call us when you want us, won't you?'

Hector steered Lucasta out of the sanctuary into the front row of pews.

'Tell me what happened about the service last Sunday,' he said.

'Well, of course, the vicar was knocking on the front door at ten minutes to eight asking why the church wasn't open . . .'

'Excuse me, Mr Hector, but could you please come and look at something?' Jenkins seemed bewildered. 'The legs of this table, sir, have got some old hole marks where obviously some brackets have been placed before. I've lined up our old brackets against them and they match exactly, and what's more, the brackets match exactly with the holes in the wall. In other words, sir, I think the table is such a wonderful match to the old one because – it's the same table!'

Hector spent some time on his hands and knees looking at the holes and the brackets and asked Lucasta to look as well. There was no doubt about it.

'Good gracious!' said Hector, remembering he was in a church.

'I suppose you'll be able to get your money back, sir, as the goods were stolen.'

'Mmm, I hope so. But he was a shady-looking fellow and I paid cash! There's no need for you to giggle, Lucasta.'

'Hector, you've been more brilliant than ever before! Listen, Mr Jenkins, Mrs Elroy only knows that Hector was bringing a table back. Now we must tell her he amazingly traced the old one to a shady antique dealer. Let's not any of us mention money changing hands.'

'Never realised you were so clever before!' said Mrs Elroy when she was told about the communion table having been recovered.

Hector looked modestly at his feet.

'You and Lucasta must of course stay until after Sunday lunch and we must all go to the eight o'clock communion service in thanksgiving!'

'Yes, very well, Mother,' said Hector.

'I suggest we go for a drive, lunch at a pub, and a walk by the river tomorrow,' said Hector to Lucasta after they'd withdrawn from Mrs Elroy's presence. 'I want to discuss one or two things with you quietly . . .'

'First, how on earth did you manage to control my mother? She's in the best mood I've ever seen her in.'

'Well, you shouldn't be surprised. You said you had a hunch about it, remember? And it just so happens that in the same way that some people are good with small children, I'm good with old people. I get them to talk about the past. Your mother showed me lots of old photos and she told me a great number of interesting things about you as a boy! Oh, and I played backgammon with her in the evenings and let her win most of the time. She loved that!'

'I see. I hope she didn't say too many bad things about me.'

'Oh no! She likes you much more than you think.'

'I see! Second question: why did you say I must have had a nanny?'

'Because you're so remote emotionally and spend such a great deal of time at your club! Next question.'

'What on earth happened last Sunday about the service?' Hector then asked.

'Well, as I said, the idiot vicar Jim was knocking on the front door at ten to eight asking why the church was locked. When he was told by Jenkins that we hadn't been able to rig up an altar and were all going to Spelling at nine, he looked a bit perturbed, I thought, but I couldn't quite understand why. When we all arrived at Spelling – Jenkins, Mrs Jenkins and me and your mum in Jenkins' car, and about twenty other parishioners in various other cars – we understood why, and I realised why he had been practising the guitar so assiduously. Instead of the Book of Common Prayer Communion Service, we were greeted by what appeared to be a rock group headed by the vicar singing *Praise The Lord* songs – all amplified greatly. I will say this – there were about thirty young people, presumably from Spelling and the neighbouring countryside, who seemed to be enjoying it immensely, but of course no one was there even of my age group, apart from possibly the vicar. Well, you can probably imagine the reaction of your mother and the others. I won't attempt to describe it. Anyhow, we were away from Spelling pronto. Your mother sat down and wrote letters of complaint to everyone she could think of, from the Bishop down through the Archdeacon to the vicar of the next group of parishes!'

'Phew! Pity I missed it! I take it your father doesn't go in for that sort of thing ever?'

'No. Hardly! Your mother eventually spoke on the phone to the Bishop himself. I think she'd rung him about twenty times by then and I suppose he thought the best way to get rid of her was to speak to her. What she said to him I don't know, but I doubt if our friend Jim got a very good write-up! But I can't see him risking making matters worse by objecting to the altar being fixed against the wall so that it's more difficult to steal.'

On Sunday at five minutes to eight the party from the house made its way across the lawn and through the wicket gate into the churchyard. It was led by Mrs Elroy, who was escorted by Hector on one side holding one arm and Jenkins on the other side holding the other, with Mrs Jenkins and Lucasta in attendance at the rear. But something seemed amiss when they entered the church. The new communion table looked very splendid back against the east wall with the cross and candlesticks on it, but the candles had not been lit and the congregation, instead of sitting or kneeling in the pews, were gathered near the pulpit, and there was a buzz of conversation like a swarm of angry bees.

'I think there's some sort of a problem,' remarked Hector.

An elderly man, presumably one of the church wardens, came rushing down the aisle breathlessly, brandishing a piece of paper.

'Ah, Mrs Elroy, please read this. We found it on the altar when we came in this morning!'

'I can't read it without my glasses on. Whatever is it? You read it, Hector. Out loud if it's important.'

Hector took the note, gazed at it and smiled. The

paper was headed: *From the Rev. Jim Wilson, The Rectory, Dimmer*. It read: *I've had enough. I've resigned from the parish and the Church and I am going back to antique dealing. I leave you to sort yourselves out, and the best of luck . . . Jim.*

Hector read it out.

'What a disgraceful way to behave,' said Mrs Elroy in a loud voice. 'Going back to antique dealing indeed! I remember he told me he'd been in antiques when he first came, but said he'd had a calling to the Ministry. I hope he was not implicated in any way with the theft of my altar.' She glared ferociously at it as she said this.

Hector pulled a face.

Ah yes, Jim might well have had a hand in it, he thought, *if he was fed up with the church being unlocked all the time and was considering leaving the Ministry. But to prove it . . . ?*

But Mrs Elroy was speaking again.

'Absolutely disgraceful! I shall report him to the Bishop.'

'But Mother, if he's left the Church, the Bishop can hardly do anything about it, can he?'

'You may be right. But I shall still report him. He should be unfrocked – or whatever it's called these days.'

But Lucasta patted her arm and whispered in her ear.

'At least you're rid of him. Let's go home and have breakfast. I really think that would be best. Otherwise we'll get involved in the discussion that's going on amongst the rest of the congregation over there.'

Mrs Elroy turned to her. 'Quite right, my dear. You're so sensible. Hector's very lucky.'

5

April 1970

'Why are you limping like that, Hector?' asked Lucasta.

'Touch of gout, I'm afraid. There's no need to laugh. It's bloody painful and nothing to do with port and red wine and all those other tales. It's a metabolic disease and hereditary!'

'Did your father have it?'

'Well, no, but I think Mother has it from time to time. Anyhow, it's extremely inconvenient as I have to go away and possibly stay overnight to negotiate a sale for some clients. And that art expert of yours has just rung up to say he has some very exciting news about the cherub painting. You know, the one I brought over from Gloria in America. He wanted me to go round straight away and see him, but I can't – I'm expected in Kent by midday.'

'Oh dear! How will you drive with gout in your foot?'

'Well, fortunately the gout is in the left foot and, as you know, the Rolls is automatic, so I shall only have to use my right foot.'

'And why are you telling me all this?'

'Well, first of all, I was hoping for a bit of sympathy, and secondly, I was hoping you would go and talk to this picture expert and see what all the fuss is about. It was you who recommended him, after all.'

'But I don't actually *know* him personally.'

'I see. I thought you did. Well anyway, you'll talk to him more intelligently than I would be able to!'

'What do you want me to do about all these books?' Lucasta indicated about two hundred and fifty obviously very old volumes covered in vellum and leather which she'd laid out on the library table.

'What do you mean?' replied Hector irritably.

'Well, I'm not an expert on this sort of thing. They're very old and I think I shall have to get an antiquarian bookseller to help me.'

'Well, get one then!'

'But on what basis? Do you want him to value the books in order for them to go to auction, or do you want him just to look them over and make an offer?'

'I don't really mind.'

'But Hector, these dealers can rip you off, you know!'

'Ah, I suppose so!' Hector was getting visibly agitated during this conversation. 'Look, I leave it to you. I *must* go. And will you please go and see the art expert?'

'When?'

'Well . . . now. He seemed very worked up on the phone just now!'

Lucasta dragged off her plastic shower cap that she had taken to wearing all the time she worked, although it wasn't really necessary any more.

'Okay, I suppose so.'

'Good girl!'

'Look, Hector, I'm Lucasta – I'm not your "good girl"!'

'Oh, sorry. Just wanted you to know I'm pleased

with you, that's all. Look, must get a move on. Jolly's having to bring the car round from the garage for me. I'm a bit slow.' And with that he limped out of the library.

Despite the painful throbbing emanating from time to time from the big toe on his left foot, Hector felt pleased with life as he drove down the A20. The Ashmolds were long-standing clients of his father and he was gratified that they had consulted him about the proposed sale of their jam-making business.

'It's all getting too much trouble, growing the fruit and then making it into jam as well,' Michael Ashmold had explained to him. 'We have endless problems with staff as the work is seasonal. I think we ought just to grow the fruit and have a long-term contract with the local jam-makers to make the jams, under our name if they want. Anyhow, there are various ways the deal could be structured. Olsens are bringing their lawyer to a meeting to discuss it all, so we'd like you to be there too.'

What a very nice and reasonable young man he sounded, thought Hector as he had put the phone down on their earlier conversation. He assumed that Michael was the son of old Horace Ashmold. Pity he didn't know more about the family background. He'd tried consulting his father's files under 'A' but most of the Ashmold files seemed to be missing. He had, however, elicited the address of the farm and discovered that it covered approximately 1,000 acres. Quite a large business.

It was a very pleasant place, and looked lovely in the April sunshine, Hector thought as he drove into the front drive leading up to a large timber-framed

farmhouse with extensive lawns around it and vast but
agreeable farm buildings in the background. A young
man approached the car as he came to a stop.

'Hello, you must be Hector. You look very like your
father. I'm Michael.'

As they shook hands, Hector thought he seemed
different from the calm person he'd spoken to on the
telephone. His face was white and his hands were
shaking and sweaty.

'Look, could we just take a turn on the lawn before
we go inside and meet the others? I'm afraid there's
been an unfortunate development, and I should like
your advice.'

'Would you mind if we just sat on this garden seat?
I'm afraid I've got a touch of gout.'

'Oh, I'm sorry. I remember your father had it from
time to time.'

'I never knew that!'

'Ah yes, he did. But look, I must tell you all this
quickly. As you know, we thought of doing a deal with
this local jam-making firm, Olsens, for them to make
our fruit into jam, maybe using our name. My old
man and my sister are the other shareholders in the
company that owns the farm – but no doubt you knew
that already – and they seemed to think it was a good
idea. But when it comes down to it, I'm the one who
runs the show completely these days. Pop's in a wheel-
chair and Sis is only interested in her showjumpers.
Anyhow, Olsens seem to have worked a flanker. Mr
Olsen says he wants to buy the place outright and has
made a huge offer. He spoke to Pop on the phone last
night. Pop and Sis are cock-a-hoop and all for it.
They're planning to buy a small place together with
some paddocks so she can do her showjumping and
he can decline gracefully into old age. They don't

seem to have thought about me. This place is my life, particularly since my wife died last year.' He swept his left arm around the horizon and then lit a cigarette with trembling hands.

'Oh dear,' said Hector. 'That's a bit problematic for me too – you see, I'm acting for the company that owns the farm – Ashmold Farms Limited, I think it's called.'

'That's right. Pop owns fifty per cent of the shares and Sis and I own twenty-five per cent each – left to us by our mother.'

'Well, you see, if there's a conflict of interest between the shareholders, each of you – or those who are in disagreement rather – may have to be separately represented.'

'But not at this stage, surely! For God's sake, can't you at least tell me what my legal rights are?'

'I suppose so,' agreed Hector reluctantly, wiggling his left foot. The pain in his big toe was getting worse and he really would have to take another couple of painkillers as soon as an opportunity presented itself. 'Presumably there's an agreement in the company's Memo and Arts that if one or some of the shareholders want to sell their shares, the other shareholders have the right of first refusal? If so, that would mean you would be able to buy your father's and sister's shares, but of course at market price, which would presumably be seventy-five per cent of what Mr Olsen is offering.'

'Bloody hell! Where could I find that sort of money?'

'A difficulty of course! But you might be able to borrow some of the money and/or bring in a new partner.'

'I've been running this place for four years now and

I want it to stay that way,' retorted Michael Ashmold furiously.

'Well, maybe Mr Olsen will be prepared to buy out your dad and your sister and you could stay on with your twenty-five per cent?'

'And be a minority shareholder!'

'As you are now.'

'But there's a big difference between having your dad and sister as the other shareholders and old Ernest Olsen. He's a tough bastard!'

'Well, maybe we could arrange for a service contract for you as managing director with an option for Mr Olsen to buy your shares at a pre-arranged price if you wanted to go. Do you get paid by your father and sister for running the place now?'

'Yes. They pay me a decent salary before we split up the profits.'

'I must emphasise that I'm acting for the company, but I don't see why we shouldn't have a discussion about all this. Would you, for instance, be prepared to stay on on the basis I've just described?'

'Oh God! I don't know. I think I'd hate it. All I wanted was just to get rid of the ruddy jam-making business!'

'Well, let's see what we can do, shall we?' said Hector, rising painfully to his feet. 'Are the others inside already?'

'Yes, Pop is telling Mr Olsen what a wonderful place this is to live in. I think myself that's why Olsen wants it. The farmhouse, you see. Well, it's my home and always has been. I was born here. And Olsen's got a hard little lady solicitor acting for him. You know the type. Smart suit, glinting eyes, blonde hair and lots of make-up. The other bloke with him is his company secretary. He's there as a sort of back-up yes-man.'

Mr Olsen was about fifty. He had a handshake like iron and an extravagantly checked sports jacket. His team were seated either side of him. The solicitor, introduced as Miss Sally Koy, barely acknowledged Hector and Michael as they came into what was obviously the dining room. She was wearing a tight-fitting black suit, a grey polo-necked jumper and a string of pearls. Her heavily lacquered hair was cut in a long bob with a fringe. Her eyes were piercing blue and indeed glinted fiercely behind her steel-rimmed spectacles.

Old Mr Ashmold was sitting at the table opposite Mr Olsen. He looked very frail. His shoulders were bent and his face was pale, and he had a hearing aid in each ear. When Hector was introduced to him by Michael, he responded, 'Knew your father well – wonderful chap . . . so amusing!'

Hector had *never* known his father to be amusing, and what with that comment and the one about the gout, he wondered if somehow he'd ever known his father properly at all.

By Horace Ashmold's side was 'Sis', introduced as Linda. She was a large, hearty-looking girl wearing a woolly jumper and jodhpurs.

Michael Ashmold sat at the top of the table and Hector sat down next to him, groping in his pocket for the painkillers when he saw that there was a glass of water on the table in front of him.

'I've told Mr Elroy the up-to-date position,' said Michael.

'Michael wants to be kept on to run the place, you know,' said Horace to everyone in general and to Hector in particular.

'I cannot allow my client to agree to that,' announced the lady solicitor.

'Why on earth not?' exploded Michael.

'In our opinion, and having looked at the place and the accounts from the last three years, we don't think it's being run as profitably as it could be.'

'Well, that's straight between the eyes,' thought Hector.

'Moreover, my client wishes to live in this house if he purchases. So it's an all-or-nothing situation, I'm afraid.'

'Mr Olsen, this all started out as my wanting to get you to run the jam-making side of the business for me, and I thought you'd agreed in principle. Now it's all turned on its head. You want to buy me out. Why the change?' asked Michael.

'Sally here advised me that it would be the best thing from my point of view, and I always take Sally's advice. I've found it very sound over the three years that she's been acting for me.'

'I see,' said Michael bitterly, and then, turning to his father and sister, 'and I gather both of you agree to the sale?'

Both nodded.

'Sorry Michael, but you'll have plenty of money. You can start up somewhere else again if you really want to go on fruit farming, but I've had enough. Linda has never been interested, as you know,' said Horace.

Michael snorted. 'You seem to have sorted all this out very well between you behind my back. I suppose you've been into the tax position?'

'Yes we have,' said Linda smugly, 'it's not too bad at all.'

'So you're determined to sell your shares in the company whether or not I agree, is that right?'

'That's correct – isn't it, Pop?' said Linda. 'Well,

we're advised that we have to offer them first to you at market price, but we're sure that you won't be able to afford to buy us out.'

Pop nodded.

'In that case,' said Sally, 'and with my client's agreement, the next step is for me to send Mr Elroy a draft agreement for the sale of the shares for consideration. I'll have one ready in the next couple of days.'

'Well, that's it then – nothing more to be done,' thought Hector. He hadn't even opened his briefcase, despite having previously thought he might be there for two days. He glanced at Michael, who looked as though he was in abject misery. He resolved on making a rapid exit and a speedy drive back to London. But as he limped out into the hall as quickly as he could, having said brief farewells to everyone, Michael rushed after him and grabbed him by the arm.

'Look, come in here for a few moments please, Hector.' He pulled Hector into what was obviously the farm office and sat down behind his desk, his elbows resting on it and cupping his head in his hands.

'It's that little bitch Sally!'

'Obviously Mr Olsen follows her advice very closely!'

'You can say that again. Christ, I'm angry! Look, Hector, I hate to ask you this, but couldn't you try and talk to her, get her to see there are other ways? What a bloody nerve saying I'm not running the place profitably! Pop and Sis must have given old Olsen the farm accounts on the quiet.'

'And would you say you're running the place efficiently?'

'Look, I married three years ago. Three months later my wife developed leukaemia. She died six months ago. Could anyone be super-efficient with all that going on?'

'It must have been very difficult.'

'In the circumstances I think I did very well, and now that I've more or less got over Muriel's death, I was looking forward to making the place really profitable again, like it was when Pop was in his prime.'

'Ah, I see – your father ran the place very profitably. Could that be a reason for his wanting to sell over your head?'

'You may be right, but I think there are other reasons too. Pop and Sis live in a separate part of the house. We made the arrangement when I got married, and as a result I haven't seen too much of them. So over the last few years, we've rather grown apart.'

'Well, I don't see what I can do to help you, although I'd like to. I don't think it would be proper for me to try and persuade your father and sister not to sell as they've made it clear they want to.'

'I know – but would it be improper for you to speak to Sally and try and get her to see my point of view? Give me a chance to make the place more profitable?'

'It may or may not be improper, but I'm sure, having seen her and how she works, she wouldn't listen.'

'Look, please try! I know she came down by train, so offer her a lift back to town in your Rolls and just talk to her, would you? Please!'

Michael sat there looking totally miserable. He was now smoking his fifth cigarette and Hector, as he often did when people were really upset, weakened, although he knew he should have refused.

'Very well. I'll have a go. I don't think she'll agree to come with me though!'

'Do you know, I could strangle her!' were Michael's final words as Hector left him in the office.

Sally Koy was still in the hall and, contrary to Hector's expectation, seemed very pleased by the idea of a lift back to London.

'Why are you limping?' she asked him as they made their way outside.

'Touch of gout.'

'Oh dear. Too much good living, maybe! Is yours the Rolls?'

Hector did not think this insinuation that he was to blame for his gout was a good start, but he opened the passenger door to let Sally in. First she nonchalantly threw her very expensive-looking briefcase and overcoat onto the back seat, and then she carefully swivelled her skirt round by the waistband so it was back to front. Hector regarded this manoeuvre with some amazement.

'Prevents bagging,' was the only explanation he got.

As he limped round to the driver's side and got in, he noticed that Sally had settled back in the leather seat, taken off her shoes and put her feet up on the dashboard. Although extremely surprised, Hector could not help but notice that she had the most exquisitely shaped slender legs.

'Like to relax when meetings are over, don't you?'

'Er. . . sometimes.'

'By the way, if you think you're going to get me to change my mind about my advice to Olsen, you're mistaken. It must be the right deal for him, you see. He wants to live in the house – he's fallen in love with it!'

'I see,' said Hector heavily. 'Suppose Michael refuses to move out – are you going to try and force him?'

'It'll be part of the negotiations. Anyway, enough of that. I gather you're a sole practitioner like me. If you ever have anyone wanting to know about horses, racing stables and that sort of thing, that's one of my areas of specialism. I'll give you one of my cards. I was a partner in a very large firm but there was a huge row and I had to leave – with as many of their clients, of course, as I could. If you think I'm hard, you're right – I am. I've had to be. I gather you just walked into your father's practice when he died. Very nice too. By the way, they gave me your address to send the share sale agreement to.'

'It's very tough on Michael to be pushed out in this way,' said Hector, doggedly returning to the subject that was still uppermost in his mind. 'Is there no compromise solution?'

'No, not in my opinion. But being forced out may buck him up a bit. Life is a tough business. I was pushed out of my former partnership. I survived. And in fact I'm happier now on my own. Perhaps Michael will be. He's been running the farm very inefficiently, you know. You can see it by the figures and looking round a bit.'

'You did know his wife had been ill and died?'

'Yes, I knew that. There are always excuses. I sympathise, but business is business. If you must know, one of the reasons I was chucked out of my previous firm was because they said I was devoting too much time to my hobby, even though I only ever did it in the evenings. These big firms think they own you and your time completely.'

'May I ask what the hobby was?'

'Ballroom dancing. My partner and I were set to be national champions before the rumpus.'

'And now?'

'Ah well, I don't have the time for it any more. I do a bit, but nothing serious. My former dancing partner was, of course, very upset when I threw in the towel, but I just told him to get a new partner. It's been a year now since I started up my own law practice.'

'Your office is in Covent Garden I see. Would you like me to drop you there?'

'Yes please. I live over the office.'

They were now crossing Waterloo Bridge, and after various twists and turns, Hector located the street in which Sally's office was. As they drove down the street, Sally became somewhat agitated.

'Oh damn and blast,' she muttered. 'Look, just drop me here would you. There's someone ahead I don't want to meet.'

Hector stopped, whereupon she leapt out of the car, pausing only briefly to swivel her skirt back in place before running up the road and disappearing swiftly through a door that must have led to her flat. On the ground floor next to the door was a large window with 'S. Koy & Co. Solicitors' in gold letters across it and a Venetian blind behind it.

As he drove back to St. James's, Hector reflected that Sally was rather a nice girl underneath the tough exterior and that her legs were wonderful. Even better than Lucasta's, he thought. But as he got nearer St. James's he noticed that his left foot, which had been quite painless while he'd been talking to Sally, was starting to throb badly again. In fact it was hurting so much as he drove into the square that he decided to park the car there at a meter and take it to the car park later, as it was a few streets further on. But as he reversed into the parking space, he noticed that Sally had left her coat and briefcase on the back seat. He gathered them up along with his own overnight bag and briefcase that were in the boot and resolved to ring Sally's office number and tell her that he'd got them. But as he came into the entrance hall, he realised that something had happened because Jolly was there waiting for him and looking anxious.

'I took the liberty of telephoning the clients, sir, and they informed me that you had left the meeting and were on your way back to London. I'm so glad you're back – Miss Lucasta wants to talk to you very urgently. She seems very worried about something.'

'Well, tell her to come and see me in my office if she wants. Oh, and bring me a cup of tea ASAP, Jolly, would you please.'

Hector felt very bad-tempered as he entered his office. He dumped the bag and Sally's coat and briefcase, removed his left shoe, swore and said to himself, 'Well, I'll never get Sally Koy to change her mind about anything. Do I tell Michael now or later?'

At this point, Lucasta entered his office breathlessly. She'd obviously run from the library and her bosom was heaving most appealingly, he thought.

'Hector, you've not going to believe this – first, the painting under the cherub is thought to be a Raphael, and secondly, I've had an antiquarian bookseller in. He looked at the books I'd laid out on the table and then he got so interested he demanded to see some of the rest. Hector, he says they're worth a fortune!'

'Good Lord,' responded Hector in a somewhat subdued way. 'Really?'

'Well, you don't seem very excited.'

'No, I just want a cup of tea and a couple more painkillers. And if you're going to stay and tell me more about these remarkable events, do you think you could speak more quietly? Shouting excitedly makes my foot hurt you see.' He pointed to his left foot that he had placed on the bottom drawer of his desk which he'd pulled out for the purpose.

Lucasta shook her head and pulled up a chair to the side of Hector's desk so she could tell him more about the things that had happened. As she did so, she noticed that his sock had a large hole in the big toe.

It was half past five when Hector remembered that his car was parked outside and that he had Sally Koy's briefcase and coat. He phoned her office, but only connected with an answering machine saying that the office was closed. He must get Jolly to move the car, he supposed. He picked up Sally's overcoat and brief-case to put them on the top of his filing cabinet, but as he picked up the coat, he noticed a delightful smell, particularly from around the collar. Perhaps he really ought to make the effort to take Sally's briefcase back to her tonight. It seemed rather heavy and might have some important papers in it that she'd be want-ing first thing in the morning. . .

When he had hobbled to the Rolls, he saw that, pre-dictably, it had a parking ticket stuck on the windscreen, which he picked off in annoyance and put in his pocket. He then drove slowly and thoughtfully to Covent Garden through the rush-hour traffic. He thought that if Lucasta's bookseller was right, his finances were looking up even though he supposed he'd have to come clean with the Inland Revenue and tell them that his father's books were worth more than the thousand he'd estimated when the old man died. And then there was the Raphael. This seemed so unlikely, he could hardly believe it, but even so, he had persuaded Lucasta to telephone Gloria to tell her the good news. Gloria's reaction he knew would be predictable. Even a small painting by Raphael, he assumed, would be worth a great deal, and no doubt Gloria would be on the first plane to London. He really didn't think he could stand seeing her at present. He parked the Rolls round the corner from Sally's office and flat in a road that seemed strangely to be devoid of parked cars. Sally's office was definitely closed as there was no light on in it, so he thought he would try her flat. He rang the bell, but there was no answer. Then he noticed that the door leading up to it from the street wasn't properly shut, so pushed it wide open and shouted up the flight of stairs, 'Miss Koy, are you there?' But of course she couldn't hear him up a flight of stairs. So he climbed the stairs painfully. They led to another door, also ajar. He knocked on this and shouted again. Still no reply. *How very odd for both the doors to be open*, he thought. He pushed the flat door open and went in and shouted for Sally again. There was silence. It was obviously the sitting room that he was in, and he wondered if he should just leave the briefcase and coat there and go, but thought better of it, as she might be ill or something. He pushed open the door of the next room. It smelt very scented in there – just like the overcoat. It was obviously her bedroom. It was illuminated by the street lights as the curtains were not drawn, and he could make out a figure on the bed. The shapely legs were unmistakable – but Sally was fully clothed. She must have gone to sleep, Hector thought. He tiptoed over to the bed, where he noticed that Sally appeared to be in a very strange position for sleeping. He looked at her face and realised with horror that it was red and puffy. He found the main light switch and flicked it on. He had never in his life fainted, but now he felt his head spinning and his legs giving way. He sat down on the bed and tried to control his body. Not only did he feel faint, but he thought he was going to be sick. Slowly, he forced himself to look at Sally again. He was appalled. Her glasses lay broken on the pillow beside her head, and from the red weals round her neck he knew that she'd undoubtedly been strangled. Had she struggled at all, he wondered, or had she been attacked while asleep? Her skirt was still pulled down, so it did not seem that she had been sexually assaulted. But one of her shoes was on the floor beside the bed. She had looked so lovely in his car that afternoon and so alive; and now she was very dead. And Michael's last words came immediately to his mind: 'I could strangle her!'

'Just sit down, sir, and tell me once again clearly and slowly how you came to be in this flat.'

Hector explained again. Chief Inspector Burke looked at him very suspiciously. Burke was a bombastic little man in his mid-fifties, balding and moustached, who obviously took himself and his work very seriously.

'I see. And you just found the street door ajar? Didn't you think that strange?'

'I did – a bit.'

'And you say you had never met the deceased before today? Is that correct?'

'Perfectly correct, Inspector.'

'It seems strange that you came home together in your car when you told me there'd been such a disagreement at the meeting.'

'Well, as I told you, Inspector, my client Michael Ashmold asked me if I would give Miss Koy a lift to try and persuade her to change her advice to her client, Mr Olsen.'

'A bit irregular, wouldn't you say?'

'I suppose so, yes.'

'And did you get her to change her mind?'

'Not in the slightest.'

'So you had a row in the car?'

'Not at all, Inspector. In fact, we got on rather well!'

'Ah, I see. The deceased is, or rather was, a very attractive woman?'

'She was indeed.'

'And you were attracted to her?'

'A little, I suppose. She was very hard at the meeting, but I could see when I talked to her that that was only her professional persona.'

'I see. I put it to you, sir, that she could have left her things in the back of the car in the hope that you would deliver them back to her later.'

'I think that is a ridiculous suggestion, Inspector.'

'Why?'

'She left them in my car because when we drove into this street, she saw someone she knew and said she wanted to avoid, so she got me to stop the car before we got to them and then she jumped out and ran to her flat door and disappeared, forgetting about her coat and briefcase in her haste.'

'Why should she do that? If she'd wanted to avoid this person she could have asked you to drive on and come back later.'

'I don't know, Inspector.'

'Who was the person she didn't want to meet?'

'Once again, I don't know, Inspector. I think it was a man. Maybe if I saw him again I would remember him.'

Hector was beginning to dislike Chief Inspector Burke greatly. He had obviously modelled himself on the fictional TV detective Hector liked least. He now

98

hovered over Hector, who was seated in a small upright chair feeling very uncomfortable, his left big toe throbbing constantly. He felt all of this was most unfair. He had only tried to do the decent thing and return Sally's things to her, and here he was being treated as a criminal!

The chief inspector had broken off the questioning for a minute or two while he shouted orders to two uniformed officers who appeared to be ransacking the flat for clues, and to some men with a stretcher who were taking away Sally's body. But now he'd returned and stood threateningly once again over Hector.

'You're sure Miss Koy was dead when you entered the flat?'

'Positive. Look, Inspector, if you think I strangled her, would I really have then telephoned for the police and waited here? No, I'd have done a bunk and been on the run!'

'In my experience, sir, criminals do strange things after committing crimes, but it's very interesting you should say what you've just said because my colleagues in Kent have visited the Ashmolds' farm and it would seem that Michael Ashmold has disappeared – done a bunk, as you might say. His sister says that shortly after the meeting ended, he uttered certain threats against Miss Koy, among them that he could strangle her. Do you recall him saying that?'

'Ah yes, he said that to me, Inspector, but I'm sure he didn't mean it literally.'

'Why are you so sure, sir?'

And so the questioning went on and on. Eventually Hector, who'd not eaten anything since breakfast time and was in pain and very tired, said, 'May I suggest, Inspector, that rather than questioning me interminably when there is nothing else I can add to what I've told you already, you and your colleagues direct your energies to finding Mr Ashmold? I am a solicitor. You have my address. I'm not feeling well, as I told you, because I have an attack of gout and I should like to go home to bed.'

Surprisingly, this speech appeared to deflate the bombastic chief inspector, who, after a long silence, agreed that Hector could go home after he'd signed a statement.

When Hector left the flat, feeling free at last and gratefully breathing in a few deep breaths of night air, he saw from his watch that it was just past midnight. He limped towards where he had parked his car – to find that it was not there! At first he thought it must have been stolen, but then he saw a large notice affixed to a lamppost which announced that road-works would be commencing and that any vehicle parked in the street would be removed. He had of course not seen it when he'd parked, although he remembered that he'd thought it strange that there were no parked cars in the road.

He was eventually able to hail a taxi that took him home. In the small and little-used kitchen off his sitting room, he found nothing to eat but a small tin of baked beans and a sliced loaf. He opened the can of beans, cutting himself neatly in the process, and heated the beans and ate them on a piece of buttered toast. With this, he had two large whiskies and two more painkillers. It had not been a good day, he thought as he climbed the stairs and lay down on his bed. But then he remembered about the Raphael, and better still, his father's old books. 'Worth a small for-tune,' Lucasta had said. He wondered what exactly 'a small fortune' was. He slowly undressed and gently inserted his left foot into the bedclothes, having taken off his shoe with some difficulty. It did somehow ease the pain taking off the shoe and knowing that the books were worth a great deal . . . but, oh dear, the baked beans were giving him terrible wind . . .

'Look, Jolly, I must see Hector. It's very urgent!'

'I'm very sorry, Miss Lucasta, but I'm afraid you cannot. Mr Hector is in his bed and appears to be very ill. In fact, I've called the doctor.'

'But what's the matter with him?'

'We think it's a very bad attack of gout. At least we hope it is nothing more serious.'

'Well, he had what he called "a touch" of gout yesterday – but Jolly, I must insist. If he's only got gout he can speak to me!'

'Can it not wait until after the doctor's called?'

'I know all about doctors calling – we could wait all day! Look, his rooms are one floor up, aren't they? I'm going to see him!'

At which Lucasta determinedly climbed the elegant staircase up to the first floor with Jolly in pursuit muttering, 'I think this is most unwise.'

'Which way now, Jolly?'

'To the right, miss. That's the sitting room and then, if you really must, his bedroom is up the staircase inside the room. But I really think I'd better go up first.'

Lucasta ignored all this, noting briefly that the sitting room was lined from floor to ceiling with bookshelves and books. It reminded her of the smoking room in a gentlemen's club in Pall Mall where she had once been admitted on some sort of special occasion. She pushed past Jolly before he could stop her, and ascended the flight of stairs leading to the bedroom.

Hector was lying unshaven and propped up in bed with his eyes closed. He opened them a fraction as Lucasta entered the room and groaned.

'Good God, Lucasta, what are you doing here?'

'I've come to ask you two things that I'm afraid can't wait,' announced Lucasta.

'Could you please speak very quietly? It hurts when you shout, as I've told you before.'

'I'm not shouting!'

'Well you have a very piercing voice then. Could you please speak very, very softly? Bring that chair up near the bed, sit on it and just whisper will you if you must say something.'

Lowering her voice to a stage whisper, Lucasta spoke: 'Jolly says your gout's worse.'

'It would appear so.'

'And it's laid you low.'

'Have you never heard the story of Pitt who, when asked to be Prime Minister, declined because he had the gout?'

'Vaguely. Look Hector, I'm very sorry you're not well, but I have two pressing problems that can't wait. First, I telephoned, as instructed, your friend Gloria, who, predictably, will be here on the first available plane. She'll be staying at the Dorchester, she informs me, and will be "right over to see you", as she put it. Secondly, the first antiquarian bookseller who said your father's old books were worth a small fortune is pressing strongly to come back with a second anti-quarian bookseller who's a friend of his and look through the whole cupboard with a view to their making a joint offer for the lot. The first antiquarian bookseller says he will have to take out a large mort-gage on his home, his shop and his stock if he wanted to buy all the books himself. Now what shall I do?'

At that moment there was a frantic tapping on the bedroom door and Jolly entered. 'The doctor is here, sir!' he announced.

The doctor was a very tall angular Scotsman, who proceeded to Hector's bedside and stuck out his hand, which Hector reluctantly shook, feebly, having lifted his right hand over the bedclothes.

'I'm Dr Macnab – I attended your late father. Nice man. Sorry he's gone. Now, Jolly tells me you've got the gout in your left foot. Let's have a look.' At which he hauled back the blankets and sheet, revealing Hector's stark-naked body. Hector feebly protested, indicating Lucasta, who was sitting about two feet away. The doctor noticed Lucasta for the first time.

'Oh, I'm so sorry. I thought you were the wife!'

'Don't worry,' said Lucasta. 'I've seen naked men before.'

This appeared to settle the matter for Dr Macnab, as he then proceeded to peer at Hector's left foot, which Lucasta could see was extremely swollen.

'Och, same as your father used to have. Gout is hereditary, you know. I suppose you're in pain?'

'Of course,' said Hector.

'Well, I'll give you a prescription for colchicene and you'd better take two of these very strong painkillers that I have in my bag. They'll definitely ease the pain, but make you feel a bit woozy. I'll give you two more for the night. Now, colchicene is an old remedy but it works well. I suggest you take three tablets today, then two a day thereafter. But you must stop once you start having stomach pains, vomiting or diarrhoea. You should be better in a few days. Never had gout before?'

'Only a few twinges.'

'You've been lucky. Here's the prescription – no

doubt Jolly will get it for you. Cheerio.' And as fast as he had entered, Dr Macnab departed.

'I thought you said it was your mother who had gout?' said Lucasta sharply.

Hector shrugged feebly.

'You'd better take these painkilling tablets now. Is the bathroom through there?' asked Lucasta.

'Yes. Should be a glass in there.'

When Lucasta came back with the glass filled with water, she watched Hector swallow the two tablets and could see, now that she was calmer, that he was indeed extremely unwell.

'Look, I'll go and get the prescription for you if you'll give me an answer to both my questions when I get back.'

'That's very kind of you. Yes, please get the prescription, but I can answer both your questions now. Please keep Gloria away from me until I'm better. To have her hugging me with gratitude while I feel at all unwell would set me back a week. Just tell her I'm ill and can't see anyone for the time being. With regard to the books, I am most distrustful of all dealers. They'll be slipping a few small volumes into their grubby coat pockets on the quiet. What we must do is this: you should make a list, as accurately as you can, of what books there are and ask them to put a price against each item and watch while they look at them. Wouldn't you agree that would be sensible?'

'That must be a good idea – but Hector, you don't seem very elated by the prospect of getting a fortune for your father's books!'

'Well, I am, of course. But the pain in my left foot is really terrible and one of my clients is I think being hunted by the police for a murder I'm sure he never committed. My mind is not clear enough now to explain it to you, but I will when I'm feeling a bit better.'

'Oh, Hector, you're not now considering taking up murder detection are you?'

'I feel I have to. I found the body, you see!' said Hector solemnly.

6

April 1970 continued

By afternoon, Hector had become so agitated by the murder – in spite of his painkillers, which made him feel quite drowsy – that he felt he had to ring the farm to see if there was any news of Michael.

'No, there isn't – he's taken his car and disappeared completely,' Linda snapped back down the phone. 'We've had police here all day asking all sorts of questions about our business and everything. Of course, we've had to tell them that Michael did utter threats against the poor girl. Well, you probably heard him as well!'

'But I'm sure he didn't actually strangle her. He just felt like it.'

'Well I'm sure he didn't either – but why has he vanished?'

'I don't know why he's vanished. Because he was upset I suppose. Look, I'm laid up with gout at present, but as soon as I'm better I'm going to start investigating.'

'Well, good,' said Linda ungraciously. 'We need a bit of help.'

If only I could feel better now and get up, thought Hector, but since he didn't, he stayed in bed and tried to think out a plan of campaign.

While Hector ruminated in bed, Lucasta, taking a break from listing all the rare books in the cupboard, was having tea with Gloria at the Dorchester. Gloria, clad in a bright red trouser suit, was enthusiastically telling Lucasta about the glories of English afternoon tea with scones, butter and jam, as if Lucasta was an alien! They sat on a small sofa, with Gloria's body-guard a few yards away, not participating in the tea, in a small armchair. Gloria told Lucasta, of course, how devastated she was about Hector's illness, how excited she was about the Raphael, and how wonderful it was to be in London again. Lucasta was able to study Gloria closely during this monologue. False eyelashes. Probably over fifty. Ridiculously enhanced bosom – it was almost as big as her own – and too much make-up. In addition to all these failings, Gloria seemed to Lucasta one of the most materialistic people she'd ever met. Lucasta had supposed that Gloria would immediately want to go and see her Raphael, the overpainting having now been carefully removed, but Gloria appeared to be much more interested in specu-lating how much it was worth and how and where she should sell it.

'Look, darling, you must know all the good dealers. Take me round them, would you, so I can see what I can get for it. If it's not enough, I'll have to take it back with me to the States!'

Lucasta wondered what difficulties would be encountered in doing this. Hector had managed somehow to smuggle an insignificant small painting into the country, but taking a known Raphael out of it might be somewhat more difficult!

'Look, darling, you must think of the best five dealers in town and then we'll get the picture tomor-row and tout it round them.'

Lucasta shuddered at the brazenness of it all.

'I'm extremely busy cataloguing some very rare books for Hector at the moment, and it's very urgent,' she explained. 'Could I perhaps give you a list of a few dealers so that you could go round on your own – with your staff of course?' She nodded towards the bodyguard. 'I will take you to meet the restorer, however. In my opinion he's done a wonderful job and no doubt he'd like to be paid for it.'

'Darling, I'll settle with him once the picture's sold.'

Two days later, after a spectacular bout of diarrhoea and vomiting, Hector was feeling better. Jolly had brought him tea and toast from time to time, which was all he wanted. The doctor had been again, at which time he indicated that Hector would have to take something called allopurinol for the rest of his life. He also apologised about his mistake about the 'young lady'.

'I just assumed, my dear fellow!'

'Quite all right,' said Hector.

And now he was getting up and having a much-needed bath and shave and fitting his left foot gingerly into his shoe. He had decided what to do about the murder investigation, but first made a call to the farm to make sure that Michael was still missing. It was 11.30 a.m., and he resolved to go to the late Sally Koy's office straight away. He would take the car. Then he remembered it had been impounded. Stopping only to give instructions to Jolly to find out about the whereabouts of the Rolls, he strode, still slightly limping, out of the front door.

'Are you going out, sir? Oh well. Miss Lucasta keeps saying she wants to see you urgently.'

'Look Jolly. it's a question of priorities. One of our

clients is suspected of a murder he didn't commit. I've wasted two days lying in bed with this infernal gout and now I must go and deal with it. I can't be in three or four places at once, can I?'

Once outside, he hailed a taxi which dropped him at the offices of S. Koy & Co., which he entered. All was very quiet. A plain young lady sat behind a desk which had a notice saying 'Reception' on it. She smiled bleakly at Hector.

'Hello,' said Hector brightly. 'I'm Hector Elroy. May I speak to Miss Koy's secretary please?'

'You're looking at her,' said the young lady.

'Ah – I see. Well, um, I'm very sorry about Miss Koy's death.'

The girl nodded.

'I brought her back from the meeting at the Ashmolds. She left her coat and briefcase in the back of my car by mistake and when I went to her flat to bring them back to her – well, I found her body.'

The girl had started to cry.

Hector hurried on mendaciously, 'The fact is that, well, at the meeting Miss Koy picked up some papers of mine relating to another case – I'm sure by mistake. She must have brought them back in her briefcase. I wondered if we could look in it and see if they are still there.'

The tears were now flowing freely.

'I'm sorry but I think the police still have her briefcase,' she was finally able to say. 'Anyway, I can't do anything without consulting him in there.' She jerked her head behind her to what was obviously Sally's office. 'He's from the Law Society, you see.'

'Oh, I see. Well, it's pretty hopeless, I think, if the police still have her briefcase, because that's where my papers would be.'

The secretary was now dabbing her eyes with a tissue.

'Er, I'm sorry you're so upset,' said Hector rather feebly.

'It's just nice to talk to somebody who knew Sally. She was an orphan, you know. I've been with her five years, you see.'

'Well, yes. That's a long time. Look, can't I take you out for a drink or a spot of lunch? Is there anyone who can take over from you?'

'Yes, there's Rita. That would be really nice – I'll go and get her.'

Five minutes later, Fleur – for that was the plain girl's name – was gulping gratefully at a large glass of white wine in a bistro round the corner.

'It's true she wasn't molested, isn't it?' she asked Hector. 'You'd know, as you found the body.'

'Not as far as I could see. She was just lying on her bed fully dressed as though she'd fallen asleep. You see, when I brought her things back, I found the flat door open and thought it odd, so I went up and there she was . . . And then I just called the police.'

'And they suspect one of your clients, don't they?'

'Well, they're so stupid, they suspected me at first. I ask you, would you call the police if you'd just strangled someone? Anyhow, Michael Ashmold has apparently disappeared, but that could be for other reasons. Tell me, did Sally have any close friends at all?'

'She didn't have any family at all that I know of and she didn't have many friends, particularly recently because she worked most of the time, you see. She liked it on her own rather than being a partner in that great outfit in the city, but it was very hard for her at first when we came here. She just worked. She even had to give up her dancing, even though it was that that had caused the row with her old firm.'

'Yes, she told me about that.'

'Tom – that was her dancing partner – was furious! They were going in for the Championships, you see, and probably would have won. She just said she couldn't do it any more and he'd have to find himself another partner, which he did. But he and his new partner didn't come anywhere in the competition. And then when she started up doing a bit with this new chap, Donald – well, there was a rumpus.'

'What sort of rumpus?'

'Well, Tom heard about it apparently and came round to the office and started shouting. She had to tell him to leave otherwise she'd call the police and all that.'

'I see.'

By this stage, Fleur was attacking a plate of lasagne with considerable gusto. 'And,' she added, 'he tried again, but *I* was too quick for him. I told him to go.'

'And he went?'

'Yes. You may not believe this, but I can be very fierce if I want to be. I am . . . *was* . . . very fond of Sally. She was only hard about work, not in other ways.'

'Oh dear,' said Hector as the tears started to flow again.

'Are you coming to the funeral?'

'I didn't know it was going to be so soon,' replied Hector.

'Oh yes. The police said it was okay.'

'Are either Tom or Donald likely to be there?'

'I don't know.'

'When and where is it?'

'Golders Green. Eleven-thirty tomorrow.'
'I'll be there, of course,' said Hector.

'I can't see Gloria this morning – I'm going to a funeral.'
'But I told her you were better!'
'Well, it'll have to be this afternoon – maybe.'
'But she's driving me mad!'
'I expect she is. She's like that.'
'The dealers all say they're not sure if it is a Raphael.'
'Well, what on earth can I do about that? She'd better get it authenticated or whatever. Can't she take it to the National Gallery or something?'
'No – she won't do that as she says if it's authenticated as a Raphael they won't ever let her take it out of the country, and that it's all your fault for smuggling it in in your suitcase in the first place!'
'Well! There's gratitude again.'
'And Hector!'
'Yes.'
'You're still very irritable!'
'No I'm not.'
'You're trying to investigate this murder, aren't you?'
'Well, yes. I'm trying to find out who killed the girl,' said Hector stiffly.
'I saw a picture of her in one of the tabloids. Very glamorous. A "leggy blonde", they described her as. Was she?'
'She was a very attractive girl.'
'I see. Well!'
There was a silence.
'Look, I must speak to you about your books as

well. I've made the list as you suggested. Is it all right to get the two antiquarian booksellers in now?'

'It is, but you must stay with them at all times, Lucasta. I don't trust them.'

'How the hell can I stay with them and deal with your daft friend Gloria at the same time?'

Lucasta's face was becoming extremely red.

'Look, calm down, old thing. Just tell Gloria I'll see her this afternoon, and put the two antiquarians off until tomorrow. I'm hopeful of maybe solving the murder by then!'

Far from calming Lucasta down, this statement seemed to enrage her even more. She said something like 'Bah!' and turned and strode off to the library. At that moment, Jolly appeared through the front door.

'I'm glad to say, sir, I've retrieved the car from the authorities and it is now safely in the garage. Fortunately, it appears to be undamaged by the experience. Here's the bill for everything.'

'Excellent. Well done, Jolly.'

In spite of the fact that he was going to a funeral, Hector felt in a very good mood. He supposed it must be because he was cured of the gout. But as he drove towards North London he did wonder why Lucasta was so cross. It must be because he called her 'old thing' he thought to himself.

Hector parked in the car park in front of the crematorium, a bleak place at any time, but now that it had begun to drizzle, a really melancholy sight. He wanted to get into the chapel before anyone else to get a seat so that he could have a good look at everyone as they came in, but his way was barred by a functionary.

'Just a moment, sir. We've just had a Jewish funeral and the chapel is being rearranged.'

113

After a few moments, the cross had been reinstalled and Hector was allowed in.

Let us hope the guilty party is among the mourners! he said to himself as he sat down. And then he thought that a prayer for Sally, as well as one for him to find out who murdered her, would be appropriate, so he knelt down, at the same time keeping his eyes open to see who came into the chapel.

Sitting again, he smiled at Fleur as she came in. She still seemed very upset. She sat right next to the coffin. Hector waited impatiently for more people to arrive, but by the time the canned music started and the clergyman entered, there were only three other men in there in addition to himself and the undertakers.

The dreary ceremony was over very quickly. Fleur cried loudly throughout and made her way swiftly to the door once it was over. But Hector intercepted her.

'Quick, who's that chap over there just getting up from his seat?'

Fleur looked tearfully to where Hector pointed.

'That,' she said, 'is the wretched Tom. I thought he would come.'

Hector led Fleur outside.

'Look,' he said earnestly, 'do you have his address at all or phone number? Have the police ever asked you for it?'

'No, the police have never asked, although of course I told them about him. But yes, I must have his address in the office somewhere.'

Hector had the greatest difficulty convincing Chief Inspector Burke that it was Tom Merryl he had noticed lurking in the street when he had dropped

Sally off at her flat. Burke was still firmly convinced that Michael had driven to London and somehow carried out his threat to strangle Sally and then disappeared.

However, the later editions of the *Evening Standard* announced that the police were questioning a suspect in connection with the murder of Sally Koy, and that the suspect was her former dancing partner.

Hector was feeling on top form as Gloria's arrival was announced by Jolly, who ushered her into his office at tea time. She was wearing a grey overcoat with an extravagant fur collar, but immediately discarded it to reveal a figure-hugging silk dress of cherry pink.

'Hector, darling,' she gushed, opening her arms to him theatrically. 'I'm so glad you're better at last. Your offices are just so cute and that old man-servant of yours . . . Well! And do all attorneys in London dress like you? You look as if you're going to a funeral!'

'Actually, I've just been to one,' said Hector, disengaging himself from Gloria's fond, long and tight embrace.

'Well, darling, it's all going to be all right. I've found a dealer at last who wants to buy the picture. He says he's sure it's a Raphael, but I must try and get him to raise his price substantially!'

'Splendid! And do you like the Raphael? I haven't had a chance to see it myself.'

'You will, you will. She's a lovely Madonna. I'm going to throw a little party around her. But do you know, Hector darling, I think I preferred the cherub with his chubby little ass. But then he was worth zilch. So there we go! It's tomorrow night at the Dorchester. And of course you and your charming girl Lucasta must come. She's been so helpful at a time when I know you're keeping her desperately busy . . . Are you and she . . . well, you know . . . ?'

'Certainly not,' replied Hector gruffly. 'She just works for me.'

Hector and Lucasta went by taxi to the Dorchester. Hector had changed into a less formal suit for the occasion. But it still had a waistcoat, and Lucasta did so hate waistcoats! Under her coat she herself had on what she thought was a very nice bright blue dress. On the way, she noticed a flysheet for the *Evening Standard*. The banner headline read: 'Sally – Man held'.

'I suppose this is thanks to you solving the case?' she said to Hector somewhat sharply.

'Ah, yes, I expect so,' said Hector complacently.

'Is your gout completely better?'

'Yes. It is. Thank you for asking.'

'You've been very, very bad tempered you know.'

'Oh, have I really? I'm sorry.'

The party was pure Hollywood. Gloria had invited every celebrity she could think of to her enormous suite and they all spent a great deal of time hugging and kissing one another and drinking copious amounts of champagne. The Raphael was displayed on a small table at the side of the room.

'You'd better come and have a look, Hector,' said Lucasta. 'I think it's lovely!'

'Um. Gloria said she preferred the cherub!'

'That's because she's a moron.'

They stood and looked at the Raphael Madonna.

'Well, what do you think?' asked Lucasta.

'I hope nobody tries to pinch it!' replied Hector.

At that moment, all the lights went out. There was of course total consternation. Three minutes later the lighting was restored – but the Raphael had vanished.

'Oh my God, my God!' wailed Gloria. 'Call the police someone! Hector, where are you? Did anyone see anything?'

Nobody had seen anything. The police duly arrived, followed shortly by a TV cameraman. The celebrities dispersed, having first done their best to be in the line of the TV camera.

'Come on, we'd better try and get some supper somewhere. There's not going to be anything to eat here now,' said Hector to Lucasta.

'Aren't you going to help the police with their enquiries about the disappearance of a Raphael?' she replied somewhat provocatively.

'No. I've asked Gloria if she insured the little picture and of course she had. So she's not going to be out of pocket. I'd like a bit of a break, I think!'

'Look, Hector, would you mind if I went straight home?' asked Lucasta. 'I had a nibble or two at the party and I'm awfully tired after listing all those books for you. I've arranged for the two antiquarian dealers to come in tomorrow and everything's ready for them.'

Lucasta had been supervising the two antiquarian booksellers in the library for more than an hour when Hector walked in brandishing a copy of the *Daily Mail*. The booksellers, who spent most of their time squabbling over what price to put beside each item on Lucasta's list, barely looked up.

'Have you seen this?' said Hector, addressing Lucasta and duly ignoring the booksellers. He pointed to the headline: 'Sally: dancing partner confesses'. 'Now I can get down to concentrating on the books and back to my legal practice!'

'Yes, I did see it,' said Lucasta frostily. 'You will no doubt tell me in detail how you solved the crime in due course. What's happened to the original suspect – the one who disappeared?'

'Oh, he's come out of hiding, so all is well,' said Hector beaming. 'Now, how are you chaps getting on?'

'It's perfectly easy to disappear,' Michael told Hector over the telephone. 'I just wanted to get away. Of course, I knew nothing of being wanted for murder. I took the cash we keep in the safe in the farm office, packed a bag, pointed my car northwards and drove all night, eventually arriving in Inverness feeling very tired. There I read in one of the London papers that I was suspected of the murder. I then stopped shaving, left my car in a car park, hired another car, and stayed in various out-of-the-way places until it was safe to come out of hiding again. I was very sad that someone had strangled the girl, but if you behave as she did, people must feel like strangling you, I think. I take it you didn't get her to change her mind on the way back to London?'

'Not at all,' said Hector. 'But what is the position now? You're in the clear and back home? Are your father and sister still insisting on selling?'

'No, it's all off. Olsen went cold on the idea apparently, so I'm a happy man again, although I think it will take time for proper relations to be restored between Pop and Sis and me. I intend to spend a few days fishing to recover. I'll fly up to Scotland. I saw a place up there when I was "on the run" as it were – nice river – a few early-season trout, and who knows, maybe a salmon!'

'Splendid idea! Wish I was coming with you.'
'Well, why don't you?'

The following morning, Hector sat in the library beside Lucasta looking through the list of books and the prices the booksellers had put by each one.

'It totals £450,000,' said Lucasta.

'Very good indeed!' said Hector. 'But could you show me this item, for instance – Number 19 on the list? *1603* – something or other.'

Lucasta went to the cupboard where she had neatly arranged the books in order. Number 19 was a small vellum-bound volume in Italian.

'£3,000. How can we tell if that amount is right?' asked Hector.

'Well, we can't, but I've just followed your instructions so far.'

'Yes, I know – good. But look, I'm going to take this one and two others to an old antiquarian bookseller I know and see what sort of price he'd give me for them.'

'I see. But does he know about these sort of books?'

'Yes, I think so.'

'What shall I tell the two old boys who came?'

'Just tell them I'm considering their offer.'

'I see – and are you going to tell me the brilliant means by which you solved the case of the murdered lady solicitor?'

'Of course, if you like. But you didn't seem very interested.'

'I was only cross because you wouldn't concentrate on the sale of these extremely valuable books.'

'You see, Lucasta, it was a question of priorities – I had to deal with gout, Gloria, the books, the legal practice, but most importantly, the girl had been murdered and one of my clients was the prime suspect because he'd uttered threats against her and then disappeared.'

'Why had he uttered threats against her?'

Hector took off his spectacles and laid them on the table.

'I'd better tell you from the beginning,' he said.

'And was Sally Koy really as glamorous as the papers made out?' Lucasta asked after listening to Hector's account of what happened.

'A very nice-looking girl indeed. Beautiful legs.'

'How do you know so much about her legs?'

'Well, she had a very short skirt on and she took off her shoes and put her feet up on the dashboard of the Rolls all the way home.'

'Huh! Sounds a bit of a hussy, if you ask me.'

'I thought so at the time, but she was all right underneath. I think she'd had a hard life. Lucasta, it was so sad when I found her lying there on the bed, dead. Tragic that someone so beautiful should die so young. The old dancing partner, Tom, must have been mad with jealousy about her new partner to have actually strangled her!'

'Very odd!'

'Well, people are.'

There was a silence; then Lucasta said, 'Yes, well, I suppose my work is finished more or less now, once you've decided how and where to sell the books. Do you want me to come in tomorrow?'

'Ah, yes, I was coming to that,' said Hector, taking a rather deep breath. 'Would you be prepared to look through Father's books in the sitting room to see if there's anything valuable there? There might be, you see, in view of what you discovered here, although

Father used to call the books in the sitting room his "reading books". I have it in mind that there may be some valuable first editions, that sort of thing.'

'But Hector, I went through the sitting room on the way to your bedroom – there must be *thousands* of books. It may take me ages.'

'Well, yes, never mind. Take your time. By the way, you've done a wonderful job so far – this library looks splendid now. All the law books in order and everything. And these piles of books on the floor are still to be sold, are they?'

'Well, thank you,' said Lucasta, blushing slightly at the unexpected praise. 'Yes, the pile of really good art books is going to be priced by an auction house. All the rest of the stuff I've sold to a second-hand bookseller and you should be getting a cheque for £3,000 very shortly.'

'You never told me!'

'Well, you've been rather busy with other things, haven't you! By the way, you'll need to replace a large number of the law books as they're out of date – I've checked. And lots of the law reports need binding. I've just stacked them neatly in date order. Here's a list of the books that need updating.'

'How very, very efficient of you! I'll have a word with Jolly about this updating and binding. Look, would it be convenient with you to possibly start on the books in the sitting room as soon as you can? I'm going away fishing in a few days' time, by the way.'

Hector took the three books to his old bookseller friend, who told him that it was very difficult to value those sort of books accurately and that he should get the opinion of one of the auction houses that had expert valuers for books. So Lucasta was engaged for two days dealing with a rather effete young man who, in addition to valuing the pile of art books, went through a list of the valuable books all over again, Lucasta having blanked out the prices the other book-sellers had put in. The young man put in two prices, one the reserve and one what he hoped the books would fetch. When the two columns were each added up, the reserve column totalled £300,000 and the "hoped-for" price £500,000.

'Just what I thought would happen!' said Hector.

'What are you going to do?' asked Lucasta.

'I have a feeling that the booksellers may be the best bet, but I'll think about it while I'm away fishing. I shall have five days to consider the best plan of action.'

But Hector was back after three days, much to Lucasta's surprise. She was at the top of the book ladder in Hector's sitting room and had by then only managed to look through one stack of the books. They proved to be nearly as dusty as the ones in the library, so she was once again clad in her boiler suit, surgeon's mask and plastic shower cap.

'Why are you back so soon?' she enquired, first removing her glasses and the mask.

'Rule one, which I had forgotten in my exuberance and due to the fact that Michael had offered to "treat" me because of my detective work that got him off the hook – never go on holiday with someone you don't know well.'

'I thought the rule was never go on holiday with a friend, full stop. But go on, what happened?'

'Well, we flew to Inverness. Michael is a terribly nervous air passenger. He consumed several whiskies in the departure lounge before we took off and was very noisy and argumentative on the plane. One of the air hostesses came over and told him to be quiet and he then proceeded to smack her bottom. The chief steward then threatened to handcuff him if he didn't be quiet, and I think he may well be charged with assault. Obviously, I found this all highly embarrassing. That was a good start. When we arrived in our hired car at the hotel, we were told that it had been raining hard for the last week and the river was unfishable. The hotel was awful and there were only three other guests – a married couple who were also frustrated at not being able to fish and who quarrelled with one another all the time, and a morose solitary man who said he was trying to write poetry and had come there for the peace and quiet! The hotel was kept by a man in a kilt. He seemed to do everything – served in the bar, made the beds and did the cooking. He insisted on telling us long stories about when he'd been in the Army, but his Scottish accent was so impenetrable we couldn't understand a word. The TV reception was so poor, you couldn't see or hear anything. So there was nothing to do in the evenings except drink and read.'

'So you didn't fish at all?'

'No. On the second day we were told about a loch in the hills which apparently had some good trout in it. I don't mind walking, but after about five miles of very soggy heather, and in spite of an Ordnance Survey map and a compass, we were completely lost. Eventually, by luck more than anything, we got back to the village – well, the hotel and a seedy post office – ten hours after we'd set off. We never found the loch. Michael rambled on during the ten-hour walk about some 19-year-old girl he fancied at a nearby farm. His wife died recently, you see. The following morning, I made the excuse that I'd had a phone call from the office, very urgent, and I was to come back as soon as I could. So here I am.'

'And tell me, what did *you* think about while you were walking in the hills for ten hours?'

'Well,' said Hector, sitting down heavily in his favourite armchair, 'I thought about you, looking just like you are up the top of that ladder in those funny clothes!'

'Whatever for?'

'Lucasta. . . I don't think I can do without you!'

'I'm sorry,' said Lucasta, slowly descending the ladder, 'what do you mean?'

'What I just said. I need you. I need you to be here.'

'And what, pray, am I supposed to do?'

'Well, just be here.' Hector seemed embarrassed. 'You know, I thought we might get married. That sort of thing.'

'I've had three proposals of marriage in my life and that is certainly the oddest one yet!'

'Well, I'm sorry, that's just the way it came out.'

'I didn't even know that you liked me, Hector, let alone wanted to marry me or "that sort of thing" as you quaintly put it.'

'At first, you see, you were engaged to my friend Duncan and, well, that was a bit difficult, wasn't it?'

'I haven't noticed you changing much since I've not been engaged to Duncan.'

'Look, I'm sorry. What do you want me to do?'

'Not be so high-handed with me to start with!'

'I'm sorry.'

'Do stop saying you're sorry. Anyhow, there's a huge difference in our ages. You must be well over 45 and I'm only 28.'

'I'm 46 actually. But Duncan must have been nearly 40.'

'That's not so bad. And talking of Duncan, there's what's called "being on the rebound", isn't there?'

'Yes – er, well, not every man would want to get married to someone who's just been engaged to someone else, especially a friend of his!'

'Do you know you're very insensitive and bossy?'

'Well, at times I can only describe *you* as impossible.'

'Impossible! Pah! That's it! I've never been so insulted in my life.'

And with that Lucasta pulled off her shower cap, divested herself of her boiler suit and, flinging them on Hector's floor, grabbed her coat and her handbag and left the room, banging the door loudly behind her.

'Oh dear,' said Hector to himself. 'That didn't go too well.'

And he sat gloomily looking out of his window at the plane trees in the square which were just coming into leaf. His reverie was ended by a tapping at the door.

'Come in Jolly,' he called out wearily.

'Sir, I knew you were back but I heard you talking to Miss Lucasta, so I did not disturb you before. I trust you had a good fishing trip?'

'Lousy, Jolly, lousy, thank you.'

'I'm very sorry to hear that. I felt I should tell you that Miss Gloria – she never gives her other name – keeps calling. She wants you to sue an insurance company for her as she says they are refusing to pay out the insurance monies on a picture that has been stolen. I had to tell her I knew nothing about it. She kept wanting to talk to Miss Lucasta. But Miss Lucasta wouldn't speak to her. She said it was a legal matter and I must deal with it. I don't think, sir, between you and me, that Miss Lucasta likes Miss Gloria much. I think, if I may say so, that there may be some jealousy between them.'

'Very astute of you, Jolly, I'm sure! Look, blast Gloria. I just want to be left alone at the moment – I've just had a shock.'

'Yes, I saw Miss Lucasta leaving the building. She looked very cross I thought, sir.'

'She was very upset about something. I'm not sure she'll be coming back. . .'

As Jolly departed, Hector thought, *The old bugger's pleased. He's back in sole control, he thinks.*

He looked at the leaves coming out on the plane trees again. *Ah, well!*

After another ten minutes staring at the trees, he rose and wandered round the room and leant against the library steps that Lucasta had been standing on. There, on the top shelf, were not only her mask but her glasses. She'd left them behind and he knew she couldn't read easily without them. He doubted if her home telephone number would be in the directory, and even if it were, with a surname of Smith it would be pretty hopeless trying to find her in it.

How had he paid her, he wondered? He left all that sort of thing to Jolly. Presumably she hadn't been on the payroll like Jolly and the cleaning lady and had just been given a cheque each week. He really must take a closer interest in the running of the practice, he thought. So easy to leave it all to Jolly. Jolly might be ill one day or drop dead or something. Since he'd taken over the practice he'd never, he realised, been down to Jolly's living quarters in the basement, not even at Christmas. He really should have. . .

After five more minutes he came to a decision. He walked down the stairs and along the hall and then turned right at the end into what was Jolly's office. It was very large and at one time there had been three clerks working in it. Now there was only Jolly, who was seated at a very substantial old desk in the middle of the room writing in a large leather-bound ledger.

'Ah, Jolly,' began Hector somewhat overheartily. 'I have to contact Miss Lucasta. I've discovered she's left her spectacles behind. I found them in my sitting room. We don't, I suppose, have her address?'

'I'm afraid not, sir,' said Jolly, not looking up.

'But don't we keep a note of people's addresses who work for us?'

'In this case I'm sure we didn't. I paid her once a week by cheque according to the hours she'd worked, as instructed by you, sir.'

'Damn! Yes, I see. Everything else all right, Jolly? Got everything you want? Haven't been in here for ages!'

'Yes, I'm very happy here, sir, as you see, and I trust that you find my work satisfactory?'

'Of course, Jolly. Absolutely first class.'

Hector went and sat in his office and looked through the post which Jolly had left open on his desk. It all looked tediously routine – and included five telephone messages that Jolly had noted from Gloria asking for Hector to 'call her'.

Sod Gloria. He'd let her stew. He had been sure from the moment the Raphael had been stolen that Gloria had arranged the theft to get the insurance money. He assumed that starring roles were becoming more and more difficult to come by and she'd be glad of some ready cash to pay for her two residences and her entourage. He'd been meaning to tell Lucasta his thoughts, but he might never get a chance to now, he reflected sadly. But there must be *some* way of contacting her if she didn't ever come back to collect her glasses. . .

He buzzed for Jolly on the intercom and dictated several letters to him. He fancied he hadn't seen Jolly looking so happy for some time as he sat there taking the dictation.

7

April 1970 continued

Considering he felt very depressed, Hector ate a reasonably hearty dinner at his club and was savouring his second glass of port with his cigar in the so-called Reading Room. In there were newspapers, periodicals, magazines and a selection of reference books. As he sat, his eyes drifted idly along the reference books – *Who's Who, List of Solicitors and Barristers, Crockford's Directory*. That was an idea! Lucasta's father was a clergyman, and she'd once said he was a canon. Now, there might be lots of Reverend Smiths, but surely not too many Canon Smiths. And he lived somewhere near Oxford. So that narrowed the field . . . He'd start at the end of the Smiths and work up the list. Feeling very pleased with this idea, he rose slowly to his feet, but just as he did so a bent figure passed in front of him, bore down on the bookshelves and, grasping *Crockford's* in both hands, carried it away with him to his armchair nearby.

'Bugger!' said Hector, he hoped not too audibly. He resumed his seat and glared at the old member whom he'd often seen before. He was dressed in a very crumpled black suit with an MCC tie and was furiously puffing a pipe, which appeared to have gone out. While he thumbed the pages of *Crockford's* he chuckled to himself from time to time. After approximately fifteen minutes of this, he nodded off to sleep with the book still open on his knees and the pipe slowly fell from his mouth and onto his chair, scattering ash in all directions. Hector saw his opportunity and rushed forward, banging the ashes on the floor with a copy of the *Daily Telegraph*. At this, the old member woke up.

'It's quite all right. No need to be alarmed. The pipe went out ages ago. No danger of fire!' And he recommenced his meanderings through *Crockford's*.

By eleven o'clock, Hector gave up. He might have to wait for the book all night. He would come back in the morning . . .

After a less leisurely breakfast than usual, Hector arrived at his club at eight-thirty and hurried up to the Reading Room. *Crockford's* was not in its place on the shelves, nor was it by the member's chair who had had it the previous night, nor was it anywhere to be seen! Hector asked the Club servant who was tidying the room where it had gone.

'I suppose the Bishop must have taken it to his room with him. He's very fond of reading it,' said the servant, shaking his head and showing some slight disapproval.

Silently cursing all clergy, Hector left the club and considered what to do. He considered a public library, but they probably didn't open until ten o'clock at the earliest. A bookshop – that was it! If one was open. He remembered there were two in Piccadilly.

After an impatient wait outside the shop, which didn't open until nine-thirty, Hector raced to the top floor, where the lady at the information desk had told him the *Crockford's* would be. He duly found the volume and surreptitiously started to copy the details of Canons Smith into his diary. Unfortunately there seemed quite a few and an assistant kept walking past him and eyeing him suspiciously. After writing down the details of five Canons Smith, with goodness knows how many others to go, Hector succumbed to the glare of the assistant and bought the book. It was very expensive.

Once back home, he took it to his sitting room out of Jolly's way, and where he had a private telephone. Starting from the bottom, as he had decided to do, he telephoned the number of the first Canon Smith. A lady's voice answered.

'Ah, hello. Is that Mrs Smith?' enquired Hector tentatively.

'No, it's Veronica Smith speaking; Mother's out.'

'Did Lucasta have a sister?' Hector asked himself rapidly. Try and see!

'Do you have a sister called Lucasta?'

'Yes. But she's not here at the moment. She lives in London.'

'*Ah, good,*' thought Hector. '*Bingo, first time!*' Aloud, he continued, 'I wanted to contact her, that's all. Do you have her telephone number or, better still, her address?'

'Yes, I do, but who are you?'

'Hector Elroy.'

'Ah, yes, I see. She told me about you at Christmastime. She works for you, doesn't she? I'd have thought you'd have had her address!'

'Er, yes. . . But I seem to have lost it!'

'Ah well. It's 410C Philimore Gardens and the phone number is KEN0024. Lucasta's okay is she? I haven't heard from her for some time.'

'Yes, fine. Well, she was yesterday when I saw her.'

131

'Good.'

'Excellent – I'm just going round to see her now. Thank you for your help. Goodbye.'

Hector, who had balked at phoning Lucasta before he set out, had only a vague idea of what he was going to say to her when he saw her, he realised, as he drove down Kensington High Street. He didn't even know for sure whether she'd be in.

In his left hand he clutched her glasses, which he had wrapped in one of her clean dusters, as he rang the bell to her flat with his right. She lived on what appeared to be the top floor of a house in a rather nice tree-lined road just off the High Street. It all seemed vaguely familiar. After a pause, a sash window at the top of a house was thrown open and Lucasta's head appeared.

'Who is it?' she shouted down.

'It's me. I've come to return your spectacles. You left them behind.'

'Ah, yes. Kind of you. Just pop them through the letterbox would you? It's a long way down. I'll come and pick them up in due course.'

'But they might break . . .' said Hector. But Lucasta had shut the window. 'Bugger this,' uttered Hector. He rang the bell again.

'What is it now?'

'They haven't got a case and they might break if I put them through the letterbox. You'd better come down and get them.'

Lucasta uttered one of her now familiar sighs, followed by, 'Oh, very well, I suppose so.'

There was a very long wait. Eventually, Lucasta opened the door a crack and held out her hand.

'Please Lucasta!' said Hector pushing the door open firmly.

Lucasta stepped back. She was in her dressing gown and it appeared that either she had had no sleep or she had been crying all night. Or both.

'There,' she said. 'You can see for yourself what a mess I'm in now!'

'I want to talk to you.'

'Well, go on then, since you've pushed your way in. Talk to me.'

'Well, not here, Lucasta. Can't we go up to your flat?'

'I suppose so!' Another sigh. 'Shut the front door after you.'

Lucasta went up the six flights of stairs very slowly in front of Hector. When they eventually arrived at her front door, she said, 'It's a very small flat, as you see. I was going to buy something bigger but then I got engaged to Duncan and stayed here. You'd better sit down. Amazing you didn't know where I lived.'

'How did you know that?'

'My sister phoned. Thought it was hilarious.'

Hector looked round the flat. It was indeed very small; really only a bedsit with a kitchen and bath-room.

'Look, Lucasta, I'm sorry for anything I've said or done to offend you, but would you please reconsider – er, well, what I mentioned to you yesterday.'

'It's too soon after Duncan. . . You're an impossible old bore, Hector, set in your ways. But I do like you. I suppose you could say you're unique!'

'You must realise I've always been keen on you right from the first. Why do you think I offered you half the reward from the Duchess? I need you to help me par-ticularly with my art-theft work – and I desperately want you to be, well, "around". It's occurred to me that there's a whole floor of my house which isn't used at all. It's much, much bigger than this place. It was the housekeeper's flat when my father had one. I could do it up and you could live there absolutely rent free and I'd pay you to help me whenever I wanted – er, well – you to help me. I wouldn't interfere with you at all, I promise.'

'Um,' said Lucasta. One day when Hector and Jolly had both been out she had in fact sneaked up to the second floor and taken a look around. There were two large rooms, a kitchen and a bathroom, she remembered. They were all very dusty, but in fact it was more spacious than the first floor where Hector lived because part of that floor was taken up with rooms for file storage.

'I don't know. I'll have to think about it.'

'Please do.'

'I'm not promising anything, just thinking, you must understand.'

'Of course. I say, you look pretty bad, Lucasta. Don't you think you ought to lie down and take an aspirin or something?'

'Do stop fussing. Please, please go away and leave me alone.'

Hector couldn't sleep properly that night, in spite of the three glasses of port he downed. He tossed and turned and eventually saw by the alarm clock next to his bed that it was three o'clock. He put on his dressing gown and went up to the next floor and looked at the housekeeper's rooms again. Yes, they could be made very nice indeed, although he hated the thought of workmen in the house as they were always so disruptive. How lucky that he'd managed to contact

Lucasta, and how strange that they didn't have a note of her address or telephone number in the office. But then he had a sudden thought. He went down the stairs into the large clerk's room where Jolly worked. He knew on one of the shelves there was a large book that had 'Addresses and Telephone Numbers' embossed in gold letters across the spine. He took it down and opened it on Jolly's desk. He then turned to 'S'. There it was, all the time, in Jolly's copperplate writing. 'Lucasta Smith', followed by her address and telephone number!

'The old bugger!' said Hector quietly to himself.

At that moment, the door opened and Jolly entered wearing ancient carpet slippers with a heavy camel-coloured dressing gown over what was obviously a nightshirt, as his scrawny legs could be seen under the dressing gown.

'Ah, it's you, sir. I heard noises and came to investigate.'

'Very good, Jolly. Yes, I couldn't sleep. You can put that poker you're carrying down. Now look, Jolly, you said this afternoon that we hadn't a note of Lucasta's address. What is this?' said Hector, pointing.

Jolly peered at the book.

'Indeed, yes, sir. There is her address and phone number.'

'And in your handwriting, Jolly!'

'Yes, sir. I must have made the entry when she arrived and then it completely slipped my mind.'

'Jolly, I have in fact seen and talked to Lucasta Smith and I hope she's reconsidering her decision to leave. I very much hope she will come back. What would you say to that, Jolly?'

'I shall be pleased about it if you're pleased, sir.'

But Hector still couldn't go off to sleep properly when he returned to his bedroom. Something – he couldn't quite place it – was worrying him. As he lay in his bed tossing and turning, outside the wind got up and it started to rain heavily. The sash windows of his bedroom began to rattle, as they always did when there was a wind. His father had never bothered with curtains. Somewhere there were two small rubber wedges to stop the windows rattling. Reluctantly, he got out of bed and put on his dressing gown to hunt for them. He looked at the alarm clock – four-thirty. He had probably only had half an hour's sleep all night!

As he located the rubber wedges and started pushing them into the window it suddenly came to him.

'My God, I must be totally losing my grip!' he said aloud. 'Of course I should have known where Lucasta lived!' He'd picked her up from her flat the day they'd gone to Norfolk to try and find the Duchess's statue. He rubbed his eyes and went to his chest of drawers where he kept his old pocket diaries and thumbed quickly through last year's to October. God, yes! He'd written her address down and even her phone number. And there he'd been pursuing bishops in the club and standing outside bookshops before they opened to look at *Crockford's*!

He sat down on the bed and groaned. He'd been warned that becoming emotionally involved could drive strong men to lose their reason and do the most peculiar things. And as he sat there with his head in his hands, and as the rain poured down outside and the windows rattled, he noticed that the wedges had dropped out onto the floor. Oh, just leave them! He knew he'd never go to sleep. He lay down on the bed in his dressing gown and reviewed his life since he'd been an adult. National service, university, law school, articles with his father, and then a short while as his father's assistant solicitor. And then twenty years with the firm in Lincoln's Inn. Goodness, how he was missing the social life he'd had there!

At about the same moment that Hector was getting out of bed and trying to wedge his windows shut, Lucasta was half asleep in her bed when she felt a splash on her face. She could hear it was raining hard, but why in her bedroom? She sat up and switched on the light. On the ceiling above her bed a small damp patch had appeared, and as she watched, a large drop of water passed her head and landed on her pillow.

'Damn and blast!' she said and got up and started to drag the bed across the room out of the line of drips. By the time she'd got it out of the way the water was coming in in a steady trickle and soaking the rug. So she started to roll up the rug, but didn't get very far with this as it was wedged under various pieces of furniture.

'Bucket,' she said to herself. Having brought the bucket in from the kitchen, she sat on the sofa and watched it fill up. Every fifteen minutes or so she had to struggle with it into the kitchen, empty it down the sink, and rush back with it. It was seven o'clock before it stopped raining.

'Well, at least the ceiling hasn't fallen down – yet,' she thought. 'I'll have to telephone the managing agents as soon as they open, but I don't suppose that will be until nine-thirty at the earliest!'

Her previous experiences with the agents during the time she'd lived there did not bode well for a speedy repair of the roof. Usually it took three or four days for someone to come and see what exactly was wrong. It was generally a very dismal bald-headed, middle-aged man in a shiny brown suit who sucked at his teeth and shook his head, and ended up by saying that he'd have to write to his client for instructions and Lucasta must understand that it might be a little while before he received these as his client lived in the West Indies. Then, when he'd got the instructions, he telephoned Lucasta to say that three sets of builders would be coming at various times to give estimates for the work and could she please be there to show them exactly what needed to be done. The upshot of this grinding bureaucracy was that last time when one of her window frames had disintegrated, it took two months to get it repaired!

Thinking these thoughts, she had a hot bath and a cup of tea, put on her clothes and a mac and went out into the still-glistening streets of Kensington. She had only two months left of her lease on the flat. It was not much of a place. She'd taken it at first as a stop-gap while she looked for a flat to buy. Then she'd met Duncan and renewed her tenancy because she and Duncan were going to buy a house together once they were married. And then Duncan had gone to China. And then . . . !

She made her way to Kensington High Street and browsed the estate agents' windows. Since the time she'd been all set to buy something for herself, prices seemed to have risen amazingly! Even with her savings and the thousand pounds Hector had given her as her share of the reward for finding the Duchess's statue, she'd need a large mortgage, and as she didn't have a regular job, she probably wouldn't be able to get one! She looked in the windows that had details of flats to let. Goodness! Rents had gone up too. Her rent was a bargain; it was sure to be increased if she wanted to renew her lease in two months' time.

'Ah, Lucasta. Nice to hear from you. Are you feeling better?'

Hector was extremely pleased that she had telephoned him.

'A bit. Look, may I come and see you?'

'Of course. Any time. No, hang on! I have a rather busy day. I've to see those booksellers at eleven o'clock and then a client at twelve, then lunch with a chap I know. And then in the afternoon I'm going to see Gloria's insurers about the picture. They're refusing to pay up, you know. So that may take a while. Would you like to come about five o'clock; I'd definitely be free by then.'

'Okay.'

'You really are feeling better?'

'Yes, a bit. I had a bad night though.'

'Yes, stormy, wasn't it! I was woken up too . . . Well, I look forward to seeing you at five then.'

The day seemed very long to Lucasta. The managing agents were more efficient than usual and actually made an appointment to come and look at the roof in two days' time. She'd just finished a very good novel by Daphne du Maurier called *The Scapegoat* and had borrowed another one from the library entitled *The House on the Strand*, which she had hoped would be as good. But she couldn't get into it. She tried the television. She switched from programme to programme, but it all seemed equally banal. Eventually she got out her knitting. She was about halfway through the back of a cardigan she was knitting her father for next Christmas. The pattern was uncomplicated, but she managed to drop a stitch almost immediately. She realised that she was not confronting the main problem: how she was going to get on with Hector. When she considered it calmly, although she'd been amazed at the time by Hector's proposal, it really wasn't all that unexpected. They got on rather well in an argumentative sort of way. And at least Hector had never tried to grope her. That had been the trouble with all her previous boyfriends. They'd all had a total fixation on her body. Duncan hadn't been much better. They met and got engaged very quickly, and after that Duncan seemed to think she'd just do anything he wanted and was most put out when she said, 'No, after we are married.' Then he'd asked her if she couldn't just take her clothes off and let him kiss her all over?

'Well, I ask you!' she said aloud to herself. And then muttered, 'What about a bit of kindness!'

And of course Hector was very likely to be rather rich in due course. She thought of his mother's large estate which he said he would sell when his mother died, not to mention the books. And she did call to mind the sight of Hector's naked body on the bed when the doctor had visited. Goodness, he was very large and hairy!

She took up her knitting again and almost immediately dropped two more stitches, whereupon she hurled it into the corner of the room. She realised she was in a terrible mood and had an awful headache. She took two aspirin tablets, put her favourite LP of the moment on very low – Schubert's Spring Symphony – and lay back in her armchair and closed her eyes . . .

She woke up with a start and realised it was four-thirty. She wanted to change her clothes to go and see Hector. She didn't really want to talk to him in her jeans and jumper. But there really wasn't time – or was there? Yes, she would change into a smart navy blue suit and take her little red shoulder cloak with her. Her headache seemed to have gone, thank goodness. She'd just have to be a bit late . . . Have to get a taxi. As she was changing, she realised that she wasn't sure what she was going to say to Hector when she got there.

It was nearly five-thirty when she finally reached St James's Square and entered Hector's hall. She'd often thought that anyone could walk in and steal anything as the front door was left open during the day and the swing doors into the hall didn't lock. She'd have to do something about that if she came to live here! Hector's office door stood ajar and there was a strange sweet smell coming from the room. She knocked and went in and then stopped.

'I'm sorry if I'm interrupting something,' she said frigidly.

Gloria, the source of the sweet smell, was embracing Hector most enthusiastically; reaching up to kiss him on his face and laughing theatrically. Hector looked more restrained but appeared to be quite enjoying it. When she heard Lucasta's voice, Gloria released Hector and turned, beaming, towards her.

'Darling, I'm just thanking Hector for what he's done. He got those ghastly insurers to pay up the whole lot. Isn't that wonderful? And I've been hammering at them for the last week and got nowhere. Look what I've brought for you, darling Hector.'

She turned and went to the chair where she'd deposited her bag, fur stole and a parcel, which she grasped and waved in the air.

'Let me unwrap it for you.'

There was an agitated tearing of the paper and

Sellotape and then she triumphantly turned and displayed a large framed photograph.

'I've signed it for you, darling – look. Come look too, Lucasta. Hector, it'll look great just behind your desk!'

Lucasta's mouth dropped open in amazement. The photo was about 18 inches by 12 and must have been taken several years previously. It showed Gloria in a low-cut but long evening dress. There was a split up the side of the skirt through which one of her legs protruded provocatively. Her head was thrown back in a wanton laugh. Across the lower part of the photo was scrawled in red ink: 'To Hector, the best attorney in the world – in admiration. Gloria Wold XXX.'

'That's me in my best role, as Ivy in *The Wildcats*, Oscar-nominated!'

'Gloria, my dear, I will always treasure it,' said Hector rather smugly.

Lucasta wondered whether he was being entirely sincere. Several rival emotions fought inside her. She'd been working herself up all day to come and have a serious talk with Hector and then she'd found him in the arms of Gloria, who now had her arm over his arm and was stroking his hand and saying, 'And darling, I'm going to take you out to a slap-up dinner at the best restaurant in this city.'

Hector released himself gently from Gloria's hold and put her photo reverentially on the floor propped up against his desk. He then looked smilingly at the American, who had taken out her powder compact and was studying her face closely to see if any damage had come to it through her recent display of passion. He drew in a deep breath and said, 'Gloria, before you get carried away and buy me a very expensive "thank you" dinner, I want you to understand that I shall be charging a substantial fee for the work I've done.'

'Well, of course, dear, I always expected you'd charge me something – but as we're such close friends . . .'

'I thought in the circumstances a fee of one half of one per cent of the insurance money would be appropriate.'

Gloria suddenly stopped viewing herself in her mirror, snapped the compact shut and put it in her handbag. She looked stonily at Hector and appeared to be making a rapid mental calculation.

'But, gee . . . that's a hell of a lot just for a couple of hours' work!'

'Gloria, I think you should consider the value to you rather than the time I actually spent persuading the insurance company. Also the fact that the ability to be so persuasive does not come overnight. It comes from many years of practice and expertise as a lawyer!'

'Well, I'll have to think about it. I don't have that sort of money with me in this country.'

'Oh, that's quite all right. As you are a non-resident, the insurers have insisted on paying the money directly into my client account, so I shall deduct my fee before making arrangements to send the balance to whichever account or accounts of yours you wish credited in the States. Perhaps you'd let me have the details in due course?'

Lucasta watched this interchange with interest as it threw a new light on Hector and confirmed her opinion of Gloria. Gloria said nothing, but the expression on her face and especially around her mouth said it all!

She gathered up her bag and fur and smiled at Hector. 'Darling, you're just wonderful!' she said, then went up to him, kissed him on both cheeks and made an exit, closing the office door rather loudly behind her.

'Sorry about all that, Lucasta,' said Hector, seating himself behind his desk. 'Now, you wanted to talk to me?'

Lucasta sat in the client's chair and said, 'Phew, Hector, you're amazing!'

'So people keep telling me!'

'And you've got Gloria's lipstick all over your face. That photo – you're surely not going to hang it in here?'

'I hardly think so!' said Hector, rubbing his cheeks furiously with his handkerchief. 'Is it all off?'

'Um, mostly. How did you manage to get the insurers to pay up so quickly?'

'Well, I shouldn't really disclose trade secrets, but I did a bit of research on Gloria. She was very well known about twenty to twenty-five years ago. She's appeared in numerous films – latterly, I deduced, of the B-movie variety. But in her heyday she was indeed nominated for an Oscar three times. Never actually won it, but obviously had clout in the industry. She's had four husbands, by the way.'

'It looked to me as if she was hoping you might become her fifth!'

'That ran through my mind also, but thankfully I'm sure she's dropped the idea after the fee I'm charging her!'

'I see. But now I've lost the thread of what you were telling me.'

'Ah, the trade secret. Well, quite simple really. Either these things work or they don't. I just had a "lucky break", as Gloria would describe it. I made an appointment with Gloria's insurers and was shown in to see some under-manager. I told him, quite frankly, that my client had been very patient with them. There was no question of her being negligent. When the picture had been on display it was in a most reputable hotel before an invited celebrity audience and a security guard was on duty. Nobody knew why there was a power failure. The police had done their best, but were of the opinion that there was little hope of tracing the picture as it had probably been taken abroad and was by now in the hands of a rich private collector. My client had paid a very large premium to insure the item and was not at all happy with the way the company had handled her claim. She was a famous film star. She would be reluctant to do it, but she felt very minded to tell the national and international media how upset she was about the way the insurers had treated her. The adverse publicity would, no doubt, reflect on the company's good name. I was asked to wait while all this was no doubt repeated to the Big White Chief, who, after about ten minutes and a cup of coffee later, appeared with a beaming smile on his face and told me that of course there had been a misunderstanding. The case had been dealt with routinely up to this point. Now he had personally been informed of all the circumstances, the claim would be met in full immediately. So I've had a good day. I even met the booksellers this morning and beat them up to £500,000!'

'Golly, you're getting rich!'

'Ah, but I shall have to pay death duties on the books and income tax on the fee.'

'But that still leaves you with a bit, doesn't it?'

'Very true. Anyhow, it's nice – very nice indeed – to see you again. What did you want to talk to me about?'

'Well, I'd like to take up your offer of living in your flat, subject to discussing the details.'

'Wonderful! I've been hoping you'd say yes. Now, what are the details?'

'Well, subject to the following . . . you'd better tell me if you agree with each point. One. I am to be treated as if I were your tenant paying rent even though you'd said you'd let me have the flat free. And I gathered you would pay the electricity and gas for me.'

'I hadn't mentioned the electricity and gas specifically, but yes, I agree.'

'Two. It would be nice if the flat, which I've had a quick look at, could be given a coat of paint and cleaned up a bit.'

'Of course. You shall select the colours and you'd better have some new curtains and a fitted carpet throughout. I think the furniture needs a bit of updating, too.'

'That's very nice. Thank you! Three. I will work for you at my present hourly rate. I don't know what you'll be wanting me to do in the future, but for the present I presume you want me to continue sorting out your father's library?'

'Yes, and there will be a lot of other things to do. The practice will, I hope, grow.'

'That's fine. What about Jolly though? I think he resents me being here.'

'I will give him a good talking to. You must understand that, apart from the housekeeper, this has always been an all-male firm.'

'I would not wish to work in the same room as him.'

'No. I won't ask you to.'

'Four. We are not to, how shall I put it, "get in one another's way", unless we mutually agree.'

146

'Okay – but that's going to be the difficult one, I think.'

'I shall be very firm about it. And Five. You are not to ask me to help on any further detective nonsense.'

'That's a disappointment. I'm sorry you think it nonsense. You have benefited considerably financially from assisting me. However, I suppose I shall have to agree, albeit reluctantly. You see, Lucasta, when you're near me I seem to be able to think much better than usual!'

'Well, you seem to have managed pretty well with the insurance company this afternoon and I was nowhere near you. I was in Kensington!'

'That's different, that's legal work. It's the thinking that's involved in detective work that I mean, you see. I enjoy it much more than legal practice.'

There was a silence.

'You don't look very happy, Hector.'

'Well I am really very, very happy that you're coming to live and work here, but I do think you're being a bit hard about the detective work. I wouldn't want you to *do* anything, just to be there.'

'You know as well as I do that it has been rather unpleasant in the past.'

'Yes, I suppose so. But anyway, I agree to everything you want. So, we should be happy with this arrangement and not be looking at one another glumly! As Gloria won't be taking me out to dinner, let me take *you*. And before that I'll raid Father's wine cellar for some of his vintage champagne. Jolly will get it out. And, ah yes, there was one stipulation that *I* should have made to you, but forgot. Jolly. I know he's a difficult old sod at times, but he worked for my father for years and we wouldn't be sitting here now if he hadn't somehow managed to keep the practice running. He's very jealous of his position. If you could possibly defer to him a little – I try to myself – it would be very helpful. You know the sort of thing. Consult him about what to do and don't give him orders. Would you try to do that please?'

'I shall try,' said Lucasta, not very convincingly.

'Now, why don't we both go and have a look at the flat and have a think about what needs to be done. How soon would you want to move in?'

'I'm not sure.'

Hector had booked a table at a very smart restaurant. This was all very nice, Lucasta thought, and she was glad she'd stopped and changed into the rather stylish navy suit she was now wearing, but while they were consuming the champagne in Hector's sitting room, and during the taxi ride to the restaurant, she'd felt distinctly uneasy. She hadn't really been honest about the leaking roof, had she? And as she started having difficulty eating her dressed crab, she knew she must tell him. Hector, who had been beaming and taking large mouthfuls of Chablis, now looked at her anxiously.

'Lucasta, is something the matter? Isn't the crab fresh?'

'Oh God,' thought Lucasta. 'Why can't I be devious?'

'Hector,' she said, pushing the crab aside, 'I haven't been entirely honest and frank with you.'

'Oh, in what way?'

'Well, I didn't . . . well, my decision to take your flat . . . well, it was influenced, you see.' And she proceeded to tell him everything – about the roof leaking the previous night and the slowness of the managing agents in getting repairs done. She thought Hector would undoubtedly be cross and that he might even withdraw his offer.

But he merely laughed and said, 'Well, we'd better get your new flat ready for you at great speed then, hadn't we? I'll write a suitable letter to these managing agents on your behalf saying that in the circumstances you must find other accommodation as soon as possible. Leave it to me!'

'Thank you. That's a relief!' said Lucasta. 'Ah! I do feel much better now that I've got that off my chest and you're not angry. I might be able to enjoy the next course now! By the way, what do you think really happened to Gloria's picture?'

'Well, I have a theory,' said Hector, lowering his voice, 'that she arranged its disappearance herself. She no doubt managed to get a good black-market price for it from some unscrupulous collector. But you would know more about that sort of thing than I do.'

'Goodness! Do you really think that's what she did?'

'Well, it's just a little theory.'

'If it's true, what a crook she is!'

'Yes, I never really liked her.'

'But you seemed to like being kissed by her. I saw you!'

'This chicken's awfully good, isn't it? I'm glad you're tucking into yours.'

'And this bottle of red wine's wonderful, Hector – but don't change the subject. You seemed to enjoy her kissing you . . . greatly!'

'Er, yes. Well, I'm only human and she's a rather attractive woman – physically.'

'I see . . .'

'Anyhow, I hope we've seen the last of her.'

'So do I. I suppose you'd like me to start work again tomorrow?'

149

'No. Looking at you and hearing about your disturbed night, I think you should take at least a day off.'

'That's very kind.'

'And I shall refrain from having a cigar here after we've finished. I think it's soon time you went home to bed – I'll put you in a taxi.'

As they stood on the pavement and the taxi drew up, Hector squashed a note for the fare into Lucasta's hand and kissed her on the cheek.

'Thank you for a lovely evening,' she said, and scrambled into the taxi.

Looking at her bottom and legs as they disappeared and as she banged the door closed, Hector said to himself, 'Oh dear – I'm having lustful thoughts about her now. Never really had those before!'

8

September/October 1970

Some months had passed and summer was drifting into autumn. It had taken much longer than expected to get Lucasta installed in the housekeeper's flat. Complete renovation of the antiquated kitchen and bathroom, which Lucasta had made it clear she would very much like, had taken some weeks and there had been the usual delays over furniture arriving and the laying of carpets. However, when she finally moved in, Lucasta had pronounced herself delighted and Hector took one last look around the flat with its alterations, sparkling paint and new furniture, carpets and curtains, all of which he'd paid for, and resolved not to enter it again unless invited.

Lucasta continued to sort through Hector's father's 'reading' books and she also took it upon herself to order all the necessary text books, law reports and supplements to bring his law library up to date and compile a proper index of everything.

Jolly was a little sulky at first, but Hector bought him an electric typewriter to replace his old manual one, and this had the desired effect of appeasing him. He seemed very pleased with the machine, although at first he had great difficulty in remembering not to hit the keys too hard!

Hector had little success in attracting new clients, but two substantial landowners whom he had looked after at his Lincoln's Inn firm insisted they wanted to transfer their work to him, and some of his father's old clients came to him with various problems they wanted his help with. He was very pleased to be able to see Lucasta every day, although they were now a little formal with one another. If he saw her going out in the evening he never enquired where she was going, although he did wish he was going with her rather than to his club yet again. He was very relieved, however, that he never saw any men going up the stairs to her flat. But his real regret was that, despite his advertisements, no new opportunities to investigate art thefts presented themselves.

However, one day in October he was contacted by the director of one of the esteemed organisations that look after the nation's treasures – castles, country houses and so on.

'I've been asked,' Hector said casually to Lucasta, 'to go and investigate a strange incident at what I understand is a really lovely country house. It's a fifteenth-century moated and crenellated hall. Part of the house is in the care of a trust, but the family still live in the other part.'

'What sort of strange incident?' asked Lucasta.

'Most unusual. It appears that a youth who was visiting the trust part of the property grabbed a very valuable small statue. This set off an alarm, but the youth ran into the private part of the house, and after being chased along sundry corridors, locked himself into a small turret room on the first floor, overlooking the moat. When the door of the room was eventually broken down, the young man was sitting in an armchair grinning. There was no trace of the statue, although the room was thoroughly searched, as was the route he took to get there. The youth has been taken into custody, but refuses to say anything. He does not appear to have had an accomplice. The police can only surmise that he threw the statue out of the window into the moat which surrounds the property.'

'Well, that must be what he did if they can't find the statue anywhere else!'

'Exactly. But why would he do it?' asked Hector. 'Vandalism?'

'Presumably he thinks in due course he can retrieve it from the moat.'

'Just what I thought, but apparently the owners of the house say that the moat has six feet of water in it and a great depth of slime and mud at the bottom and the statue would have sunk into that.'

'I see. So it would be very difficult to retrieve!'

'Yes, very.'

'But I take it the statue is very valuable and presumably, like all these things, uninsured, so it would be worth the trust's while to drain the moat to look for the statue,' said Lucasta brightly.

'Yes, but apparently it's extremely expensive to drain the moat. It means pumping the water out onto the fields nearby. And then there's the question of delving into the mud to find the statue, which is only about nine inches high. They don't want to go to all that trouble unless they're sure it's in a particular part of the moat, or indeed that it's in the moat at all!'

'Have they thought of getting frogmen to look for it?'

'I think the idea has been considered but thought impracticable. The trust, I'm delighted to say, heard of my name from the Duchess of Mercia, who is on the board of governors, and before going to all the expense of draining the moat and so on, they have asked me to investigate. It must be good news for me to have the trust as a client!'

'Well, I'm pleased for you!'

'Look, I don't want you to do anything, but I wondered if you would like a short break away. We could put up at a local hotel, in separate rooms of course, and you could look at the house and explore the countryside while I do the investigation.'

'Well, that might be quite nice. Where is the house?'

'In Norfolk.'

'Oh God, no!'

'But at the other extreme side of the county from the Broads. Very nice countryside. I went shooting there once. So no talk about going back to Grimes' pub to retrieve your jumper or whatever. It's probably at the bottom of the river by now anyhow.'

The hotel that Hector had booked himself and Lucasta into near 'The Moated Grange', as Lucasta kept referring to it, looked very pleasant from a distance in the spring afternoon sun. It was a country house by a river. However, as they drove past the front of the house, they came to an immense car park screened from the road by a tall hedge of *Cupressus leylandii* and packed with cars!

'Good Lord!' said Hector. 'The place doesn't look big enough to take that number of guests!'

But it emerged as they spoke to the woman on the reception desk that the country house itself merely contained one of the dining rooms, a lounge, a bar and a few bedrooms. The bulk of the bedrooms, the conference room and the indoor swimming pool were in a modern building off the car park behind another immense hedge of *leylandii*. Their bedrooms were, of course, in the new block.

'I don't think I like this place very much,' said Hector surveying his box-like room. 'Typical of new hotels!'

'Nor do I,' said Lucasta, 'but I shall try to make the best of it as I'm on a holiday treat, as it were. I saw a notice pointing to a swimming pool. I shall go for a swim!'

'Good Lord, I didn't know you swam!'

'Oh yes, every weekend. I always pack a costume just in case. And Hector, please, do stop saying "Good Lord"! If you really don't like it, no doubt you can find another hotel for tomorrow. I take it you have not packed your swimming things?'

'Certainly not! I'm going to take a preliminary look at the scene of the crime. It's only about five miles away.'

'How did you get on with your investigations?' asked Lucasta that evening above the din that hit them as they reached the bar through the crowd of besuited young men. It was obviously a business conference and the delegates were all in the bar. They were 'male to a man', as Hector remarked to keep his spirits up.

'Two gin and tonics please, barman. Good Lord, I can hardly hear myself think!'

'It will quieten down in a minute or two, sir,' said the barman. 'This lot are going into another room to have dinner.'

'Thank God for that! How long does this conference go on for?'

'Another two days, sir. It's our biggest do of the year. The guv'nor loves it, it's very profitable!'

'Of course!'

After about ten minutes, during which Hector stood by the bar and refused to speak to Lucasta, who seemed to think the whole thing very funny, the din was hushed by a clanging bell and the delegates were told that dinner was served. They shuffled out with much laughter and Hector and Lucasta were able to have a second gin and tonic in relative peace, sitting down among the wreckage of glasses and bottles.

'Well, I repeat, how did you get on?' asked Lucasta.

'Ah yes. I've had a reconnoitre. I'll tell you more in the morning. We're leaving this place – "checking out early", I believe they call it. Sorry to deprive you of your swimming pool!'

'Don't worry about that,' said Lucasta. 'I didn't enjoy it very much. One of those men on the conference propositioned me!'

'Good Lord! Well, I expect you look very nice in your swimming suit!' said Hector, looking thoughtfully at a very bad reproduction of Constable's *Haywain* on the wall. 'What on earth do these chaps say when they do that sort of thing?'

'Well, just what you said: "You look very nice in your swimsuit", but "the chap" added, "I'm sure you'd look even nicer in your birthday suit. Fancy showing me?" I just ignored him.'

Next morning, Lucasta tried to disassociate herself from Hector as he explained very bad-temperedly to the receptionist his reasons for wanting to leave early. The proprietor was called and he appeared to be unimpressed by Hector's complaints and insisted that he should pay for another night as he had booked for three. At this stage, Lucasta left by the front door . . .

Hector joined her by the car after about five minutes looking very red in the face.

'Do you know what finally clinched it? I told him exactly how you'd been insulted in the swimming pool!'

'Oh good. Well, that's settled then. What do we do now?'

'I'm worried that as it's Friday we may not find accommodation if we leave it till late, so I suggest we drive to the market town nearby and make enquiries. What we need is a nice quiet hotel.'

A quarter of an hour later, Hector parked the car in the large market square of the town. It was obviously not market day as the square only contained parked cars.

'Look, I see a Tourist Information Office. I shall make enquiries over there. You stay in the car.'

Ten minutes later he returned.

'They recommended a very nice little hotel, which I had a look at, and it'll do us fine. But before we push off, I must have a quick look at the church. They tell me it has a hammer-beam roof. Come on – it's wonderful apparently!'

Hector then delved into the boot, produced a pair of binoculars and marched across the market square. Lucasta followed as she was getting rather bored sitting in the car.

'Shouldn't you be getting on with looking at the Moated Grange?' she said to Hector as she joined him. He was craning his neck and peering upwards at the roof through his binoculars.

'It's a *double* hammer-beam roof!' he exclaimed. 'Look at all those carved angels!'

'But Hector, shouldn't you be getting on. . .?'

'It is somehow refreshing to the mind, after that

awful hotel, to find a nice one and then to see this magnificent roof. I have not been able to think clearly up until now!'

'And I suppose you've solved it?'

'Not quite. But I have a few ideas. Let's proceed to what you call the Moated Grange. It's a stunner! You don't have to do anything, just look at the outside first, and then you'll be able to see the inside later.'

The Moated Grange, Lucasta thought, was indeed a stunner. It dated from 1497, the guidebook said. It still stood with its magnificent gatehouse as it must have done for the last five centuries, with its mellow red bricks glowing in the sunshine.

'First, I want to walk round the left-hand side and show you the window of the room where the youth was caught.'

'Why have you still got your binoculars round your neck?'

'I brought them with me for the express purpose of looking for something!'

'What?'

'I'm not sure yet, or indeed if it'll be visible even with these binoculars.'

'Goodness it's cold out here! What a biting wind, and it's only October – it brings tears to the eyes.'

'Ah, that's Norfolk for you – nothing between you and the North Pole except sea! Why don't you run up and down the bank of the moat for a few minutes to get warmed up while I do a detailed reconnaissance with these glasses? Then we'll go inside the house. You'll be out of the wind there!'

As they approached the house, they were met in the courtyard by the trust manager whom Hector had met the previous day. He was an eager, bespectacled young man with a badge which said "Manager" pinned to the lapel of his jacket. Hector introduced Lucasta as his assistant, at which she pulled a face.

'Well, have you any further ideas, Mr Elroy?' asked the manager.

'Yes, one or two, but first would you please take me slowly from the place where the statue was stolen down the various corridors to the room where the thief locked himself in? Am I right in surmising that he was a local lad?'

'Indeed, yes!'

'Had he been seen visiting the hall several times previously?'

'We get many visitors, but yes, two of the attendants think they've seen him before more than once.'

'Ah, good!'

They were led by the manager into a very beautiful library on the ground floor.

'This is the exact spot where the statue stood,' he said, indicating a small table at the side of the room between bookshelves. 'And here's a picture of it. Virgin and child, as you see, probably fifteenth century, Flemish, stone, beautifully carved and painted. The base was attached to a wire alarm. The youth cut through the alarm wire with a pair of wire cutters, but it still thankfully set the alarm off. Now, if you'd like to follow me . . . the thief dashed out of the library and up this narrow flight of winding stairs . . . into this room above, where the man on duty did not realise what had happened. He heard an alarm ringing, but the youth hid the statue under his coat, it seems, and walked through very casually, and then went through the door over there which says "Private" and leads to the part of the house occupied by the family and not open to the public. Unfortunately, the attendant in the library is elderly and lame – we have to rely on volunteers for the job, as you probably know – and it took him about two minutes to follow the youth up the stairs and alert the man on duty in this room, which we call the State Bedroom, as to what had happened. Both immediately gave chase down the private corridor.'

And here he led them down a narrow passage with rooms leading off it on the right-hand side. 'They apparently heard the thief's footsteps ahead as he ran along this side of the house and across the rear, and finally they heard the door slam and the key being turned in the turret room.'

'I see,' said Hector. 'He could presumably have dodged into any of the rooms opening off this passage and secreted the statue in them?'

'He could. There was sufficient lapse of time and it is strange that the attendants heard his footsteps ahead. One would have thought that he would have been too far in front of them for that. But we have searched the three bedrooms and the bathroom off this passageway most thoroughly and can find no trace of the statue. The passage the thief went along at the rear of the house has no rooms off it. It has small lancet windows starting eight feet high up the wall and ends in the turret room. I'll show you.'

'I think the reason they could hear the footsteps was because the floors are of stone and he wasn't too far in front of them,' remarked Hector as they walked along the passage at the rear of the house.

'Ah, you may be right! And here is the turret room where he locked himself in. As you can see, we haven't mended the door yet.'

Hector and Lucasta looked into the room. Apart from the armchair in which the youth had been found sitting and a table, it was completely empty of

furniture, but the walls and ceilings were nicely decorated in the Victorian Gothic style. Hector opened the
small window and looked down into the moat.

'I see nothing significant here,' he said. 'Let us
retrace our steps.' And they walked back down the
rear corridor. 'There is no conceivable hiding place
here, is there?'

'None that we can see,' said the manager.

'Do you want me to search the bedrooms and the
bathroom again for you?' asked Hector.

'Well, I think it would be a waste of time. But I will
show them to you, of course.'

So they went into each of the three bedrooms and
one bathroom. The bedrooms were identically sparsely
furnished with an old four-poster bed, a large ward-
robe and dressing table and a chest of drawers.

'For guests of the family, you will gather.'

'Yes,' said Hector as he peered out of the window of
each one.

He didn't linger in any of the bedrooms, but the
bathroom he apparently found more interesting. It
was a vast room with an enormous enamelled bath in
the middle of it. It had a large bay window overhanging the moat. The window was glazed with mottled
glass and covered with a series of blinds. Hector lifted
a blind, opened one of the casements and looked
down onto the moat below. Then he peered carefully
round the sides of the window and at the window
ledge. At one stage he leant out so far that Lucata
thought there was some danger of him falling into the
moat. However, he managed to pull himself back into
the room.

'Thank you,' he said. 'I must go off and think about
all this somewhere quietly!'

'Yes, well, please take your time. We're not open to visitors today, so you'll be undisturbed.'

'Well, what are you going to do now?' asked Lucasta when they were outside.

'I have of course – as has everyone – been looking in the wrong place. Follow me.' And he set off round the right-hand side of the house. 'That must be the bathroom window, mustn't it? The one sticking out over the moat. It couldn't have been a bathroom originally when the house was built. They didn't have bathrooms in 1497, did they?'

'No, I'm sure they didn't,' said Lucasta.

'Well, anyhow, that's irrelevant! Now, let me look carefully through these binoculars. I do hope I'm not going to be disappointed!'

'What on earth are you looking for?'

'Ah! I think I see it. How very cunning!'

'Please tell me what you can see.'

'All will be revealed when we get back inside, I hope. But no, I'm not as athletic as our young thief. I fancy it will be better to ask if we can borrow that rowing boat I see moored over there.'

After about five minutes, it was arranged that the manager would row Hector and Lucasta across the moat to the house, although he obviously thought it was an odd request.

'Can we just stop here? I hope I can explain,' said Hector. 'If you could just let the boat drift . . . If you will look carefully to the left-hand side of the bathroom window, where the brickwork overhangs the moat, you will I think see a piece of nylon fishing line hanging down the wall and going into the moat. As the boat drifts past the window, I think we shall find that the nylon is fixed to a nail or hook just under the overhanging brickwork so as not to be visible to anyone looking out of the window. Ah! As I thought! Yes, there's a substantial old nail in the brickwork. Have you any idea, sir, why there is an old nail there?'

'None whatsoever,' said the manager, resting on his oars.

'Nor have I,' said Hector. 'But undoubtedly our young criminal somehow knew about it. Now, if you can please propel the boat over near the nylon, I shall endeavour to retrieve from the moat whatever is on the end of it.'

This manoeuvre proved difficult and Hector became rather rude about the manager's efforts to navigate. However, at the third attempt, Hector was able to get his hand on the fishing line, and with Lucasta steadying the stern of the boat against the wall of the house, began to haul the line in gently.

'I do hope there isn't just an old brick or something at the end!' thought Lucasta. 'We shall look very foolish!'

But no! What undoubtedly was the missing statue covered in mud finally came to the surface at the end of the line, much to Lucasta's relief.

Hector beamed. 'The thief must be a fisherman,' he said, examining the knot which secured the statue to the nylon.

'But, do you mean that the fishing line has been there all the time and none of us have noticed it?' gasped the manager.

'That was because you were all looking for the statue in the wrong place!' said Hector.

'The trust is extremely grateful to you,' said the manager fifteen minutes later when they were inside the house again and in his office. The statue stood on his desk looking extremely dirty and damp, but no doubt it would dry out and clean up reasonably well, thought Lucasta.

'The young criminal is obviously very clever and probably set on a life of crime,' said Hector. 'However, for the moment, we have foiled him. You see, I'm sure he planned it all in advance. He knew there was a large nail under the bathroom window and I have no doubt he sneaked into the private part of the house on one of his previous visits to work out the position of all the rooms.'

'They are all shown on a plan in the guidebook anyhow!' said the manager.

'Ah well,' said Hector, 'that made it even easier for him. The difficult part would have been leaning out of the window over the projection, as I found out, and fastening the end of the fishing nylon to the nail once he'd secured the statue to the other end and flung it into the moat. No doubt he intended to come and collect it by swimming across the moat as soon as he was released from custody.'

'It's amazing!' the manager said. 'I've phoned Head Office and they are overjoyed. They can hardly believe it!'

It was quite late in the afternoon when at last Hector and Lucasta got away from the effusive manager and various other members of staff.

'Well,' said Lucasta, 'clever old Hector! You really love doing this detection work, don't you?'

'Of course I do, much more than legal work. It's a pity you're so against my doing it.'

'It's not that I'm against *you* doing it – I just got fed up with the unpleasantness it seemed to entail.'

'But this one wasn't unpleasant!'

'I realise that. But it was rather chilly, and now I think a hot bath is called for. Perhaps you could take us to the new hotel?'

Lucasta was standing by her suitcase admiring the floral display in the hall of the hotel, which had a small reception desk in one corner, when she was aware that there was some terrible trouble between Hector and the receptionist.

'But I was told by the young man whom I saw before that it would be quite all right and there would be plenty of room!'

'Well, I'm very sorry, sir, but we've only got one double-bedded room left for the night. It's a very lovely room. Our best room in fact. I'm sure the young lady will love it when she sees it.'

'But we wanted two single rooms. That's what I asked for.'

Hector was very red in the face as he came over to Lucasta.

'Well that's it – we'll have to drive back to London, I'm afraid.'

'Isn't there another hotel on the other side of the square?'

'Yes, I saw it when I went to look at the church, but it had a big notice on the door saying "No vacancies". It looked a rather down-market sort of place, too. I don't think there is likely to be another decent hotel around here.'

They were both seated in the car and Hector was about to start the engine when Lucasta laid her hand on his sleeve and said, 'Hector, you know, if you'd like to ask me again now to marry you, I'd say yes.'

Hector didn't move for some time. Then he turned

with an amazed expression on his face and said, 'Good Lord, do you really mean that?'

'Do stop saying "Good Lord"! Of course I do.'

'Why the sudden change?'

'Well, it hasn't been sudden. I've been thinking it over for some time and I wondered, wouldn't it be nice to take that double room for tonight?'

'Good Lord! What, er, you mean before we get married?'

'Of course. No doubt my father will perform the ceremony, insisting on much pomp and fuss in due course. But he's always maintained, and God knows how many times I've heard him say it, that the bride and groom marry one another and the Church just blesses their marriage and registers it.'

Hector seemed dumbfounded, but eventually said, 'Well, I suppose that's right. Never thought about it before.'

'So, well, you'd better get out of the car and into the hotel and grab that room before anyone else books it.'

The double-bedded room was very nice indeed. Lucasta almost immediately disappeared into the bathroom and Hector sat down in the armchair to read *The Times*, which he'd not really had a chance to look at that day. Normally he would have smoked a small cigar, but he thought he'd better not as Lucasta would be sleeping in the room and might not like it.

After what seemed a very long time, long after he'd finished *The Times*, Lucasta emerged from the bathroom in her underwear.

'I'm sorry, Hector, they don't seem to give you bathrobes here and I didn't bring one with me. But I suppose you'd better get used to seeing me in my underwear!'

'Good Lord!' said Hector, standing up and gulping. 'Er . . . but you look lovely in it. It, um, shows off what a wonderful figure you have.'

'Now don't start getting excited, Hector. It's your turn in the bathroom, and I should like a good dinner before anything else!'

Hector insisted on ordering a bottle of champagne in the bar, followed by a very expensive bottle of wine with their dinner, which fortunately was excellent. Lucasta noticed that he didn't say much throughout the meal, just kept smiling at her and touching the ends of her fingers across the table. Towards the end of the meal he said, 'Do you know, I've never kissed you except once on the cheek!'

'Well, possibly you can make up for it soon!'

Next morning at breakfast Hector was disposed to be very jovial and was surprised that Lucasta was looking so solemn.

'Look, Hector,' she said, 'I want to have a serious discussion with you. I don't want to disrupt your way of life when we get back to London. If you want to go on sleeping in that funny little bedroom of yours and smoking in your sitting room and going to your club for lunch and dinner, I'll just get a double bed for my bedroom, shall I, and maybe you'd like to have breakfast with me sometimes. I often boil an egg!'

'Goodness, you don't mean you've changed your mind about our getting married, do you?'

'Oh no, of course not. I just thought you might want to carry on as you used to, at least some of the time.'

'Well, it's very kind of you. Yes, I suppose I should

find it a bit odd being in your flat all the time. You could always come and sit in my sitting room. It's got a nice fire in it generally. Well, you know that of course.'

And later, while they were on their way to London, he said, 'Look, couldn't we just go off and get married quickly and quietly at some Register Office? I think that would be much the best thing to do.'

'I had considered that, Hector. But I don't think it will do. Your mother would no doubt say that getting married in a Register Office was sacrilege and blasphemy all at the same time. And my parents would be mortified, although they know I'm an atheist.'

'Oh, are you?'

'Yes, aren't you?'

'No, I don't think so.'

'Look, anyhow, I think we ought to have a church wedding in a few weeks' time. I'll ring Dad and organise it, and you'd better tell your mother.'

'You know I'm still a bit worried about my finances.'

'Why on earth? You sold all the books for a lot of money and you got that big fee from Gloria. And I suppose your mother will pop off one of these days!'

'I know, and I've got an income of my own, but you see I was used to a rather large salary from my old firm in Lincoln's Inn. When I decided to give in my notice to them and take over the old man's practice, I hadn't quite realised how run-down it was and how little money the old man would leave me. I can't imagine what he did with it all, apart from buying all those books. The practice was very profitable when I worked with him. You know, I don't like the idea of having a wife without being able to support her properly.'

'Well, you are more or less supporting me already.'
'Well, it's not the same as being married to you.'

It seemed very odd for them both when they arrived at St James's Square. It was a Saturday, so the office was not open and Jolly was presumably lurking in his basement. Lucasta would have usually been out somewhere and Hector would have been at his club (which fortunately opened at weekends) or away with any of the friends of his who hadn't been clients of his firm in Lincoln's Inn. Not quite knowing what to do with themselves, they sat down in Hector's sitting room and Hector lit the fire which had already been laid by the cleaner.

'By the way, have you come across anything at all remarkable among my father's books in here yet, Lucasta?'

'Well, I'm only halfway through as I've been spending several hours a day trying to get your law library up to date. The books in here are, as your father correctly described them, mainly "reading books", quite nice, routine stuff. Sets of Dickens, Scott, Thackeray, etcetera, and innumerable novels of the type that I would describe as "yesteryear" – Hugh Walpole, for instance. Then there are history books and general books, some quite strange and interesting. Haven't you ever noticed their titles?'

'My dear, I can honestly say that since I've lived here I've never taken a single volume off these shelves – that's why I'm so ignorant about them. I brought a large number of books with me from my old flat, and they're in a bookcase in my bedroom. I'm a fan of Trollope, and I'm reading my way through him. As he wrote about fifty novels, it will keep me occupied for some time. None of the books in here have, up to the present, drawn me to open them. Look at this, for instance,' he said, taking a volume at random from near the fireplace, where he was tending the fire. '*Butterflies and Moths*, by W.E. Kirby. And next to it, *British Birds in Their Haunts*, by the Reverend C.A. Johns. Funny, they don't seem as dusty on top as the others – and what the hell is this?' he said, peering at the side of the chimney stack that had been revealed when he had pulled out the books. 'Good Lord, it's a wall safe – and it's got a combination lock.'

'Oh.'

'Well, I suppose I'll have to get it opened. It may contain something important. I never knew it was there!'

'Why don't you try a few numbers. I think there are usually four. First go clockwise, then anti, then clockwise, and then anti.'

'Oh no, it could take all day. I'll get someone to come and open it on Monday morning. Safemakers must know what to do if you lose the combination.'

'Well, I don't know. Oh, do go and have a try at opening it! It can't do any harm. Meanwhile, I'm going to make us some tea. Do you have any in your kitchen?'

'Oh yes, and there's milk in the fridge. The cleaner will have left some. She comes on a Saturday morning. Though you said you didn't want her doing anything in your flat, you remember?'

Lucasta was gone for some minutes while Hector bent down and fiddled with the combination.

'Look, I've found some fresh sliced bread in your fridge,' she called out from the kitchen. 'I suppose the cleaner lady bought that too. You have got her well organised, I must say! I've made the tea and I'll do us some toast in front of the fire. It's just about hot enough now for toasting. It's jolly funny-smelling tea you've got. What sort is it?'

'Keemun.'

'Mmm, I see. I could only find butter, no jam. How are you getting on?'

'I'm not, and my back is getting sore.'

'Well, kneel down, you'll find it easier – and be logical about the numbers. Try your father's birthday first and then your mother's and then yours.'

Hector knelt down and rather unenthusiastically started twiddling the combination dials while Lucasta started toasting the bread. After a minute, however, she jumped with surprise when Hector cried out in astonishment, 'I've done it. It's open!'

'Well done! What date was it?'

'I can't remember.'

'And it's empty, I suppose?'

'No, it's full of rolled-up banknotes. Good Lord!' said Hector, throwing three or four rolls onto the carpet. 'And what is this? This looks even more interesting. Yes, these are notices of deposits with a Swiss bank – a whole wodge of them. Heavens, this first one must be the equivalent of about twenty thousand pounds, and this one about ten thousand, and there are ever so many more!'

'And Hector, so many bank notes that I think you could stop worrying how you're going to support me!'

'Goodness, Lucasta, I'm so relieved about this!' said Hector. 'And so pleased that we're going to get married. Well, I suppose we are already according to your father.' And with that he crawled over to Lucasta.

'Hector, please don't get overexcited! I really don't mind you kissing me when I'm on my knees trying to toast a piece of bread, but you're pushing my hair into the butter dish . . . Oh no, Hector, no. Don't you think we ought to count up the money first? . . . I mean, Jolly might come in. No, Hector. I really think we ought to count the money first. Please, please, Hector, the tea will get cold!'